CAMP NIGHTMARE

PART OF THE MIDNIGHT LIBRARY COLLECTION

JOHN T. HAAS

BLACK LANTERN PRESS

Legal Deposit, Library and Archives Canada, April 2026.

First Edition, Paperback ISBN: 987-1-0675280-0-3 Ebook ISBN: 987-1-0675280-1-0

Black Lantern Press

www.blacklanternpress.ca

contact@blacklanternpress.ca

You're doomed! You're all doomed!

Crazy Ralph - Friday the 13th (1980)

INTRODUCTION

This introduction is to pre-emptively answer a few questions. You see, I did work at a summer camp—Camp Amy Molson—between the years of 1985 and 1994. It was, quite frankly, the best job I ever had in my life, and I have had a *lot* of jobs. It wasn't easy by any means, but it was worthwhile.

First important thing I will say is that I have based Camp White Bear geographically on Camp Amy Molson from back in the summers when I worked there. There's been a great many changes since then, and current staff probably wouldn't even recognize the layout of the buildings in this book compared to current reality.

Second thing important thing is that NONE OF THESE CHARACTERS ARE BASED ON ANYONE LIVING OR DEAD. Seriously, no friends or enemies made it into the book. If you *do* see yourself in one of my characters, I would suggest it's kind of like astrology. If you see yourself in the stars, it's because you want to.

I will now apologize to everyone who believes in astrology. I personally don't, but if it helps in your day-to-day struggles, more power to you.

Okay, a couple of the characters have small bits based on me (don't worry, I asked myself if it was okay, and told myself it was fine). Most notably Theo (I got in shit for telling horror stories to my kids one summer).

CHAPTER

ONE

Patrick stepped from his rental car and stood in the small lot, orienting himself. The space was big enough for eight cars, and a rusted beater had already taken the first spot, informing him they weren't the first ones to arrive. Nick exited from the passenger side and came around where he could get a better view. A cool fall wind blew around them and Nick slipped his hands into the pockets of his wind breaker.

The two were immediately overcome by a deep sense of nostalgia.

"Holy shit," Patrick muttered.

"It hasn't changed. Not a bit."

In the twenty summers since they'd worked the cabins had been repainted, just a different shade of white than their memories. The grass was more full and lush, including that perpetual bald spot around the flagpole.

Little changes.

Cabins remained the same wooden, one-room structures with a little porch... at least the ones up here at the entrance. The flagpole still rose into the sky with its Canadian flag flapping in the late-September breeze.

"Camp White Bear," Nick breathed.

Patrick laughed.

"What?" Nick asked.

Camp White Bear—often referred to simply as The Bear.

"Just remembering some of the names we called it."

"You mean like Camp White Hot in the middle of July?"

"And Camp Black Fly when the pests came."

"Camp Nightmare. Of course."

"That was Theo I think, or one of the campers who lived for his stories."

Nick returned his attention to the cabins and lawn spreading out ahead of them. "Junior boys, right?"

Patrick nodded again.

The younger boys were up here with junior girls just behind. These would have been the six to eight year olds. Senior boys and girls were further back and held the older eight to ten year olds.

"It's like time travel," Nick said.

"Closest we'll ever get."

Patrick and Nick had stayed in touch over the two decades since working here. Unbelievably it had been ten years since they'd been together in the flesh. Patrick lived in Calgary working in oil and gas. He'd flown in a day early and stayed with his old friend—a gym teacher in Ottawa—before making the hour drive to camp near the Ontario-Quebec border.

They stepped forward like two people in a dream.

"It feels like coming home," Nick said.

"Or finding a piece of yourself you hadn't realized was missing."

The part they stood on was the highest point at camp and the only entry from the road.

"The... upper compound?" Nick said. "Is that what this was called?"

"Yep."

The office stood to their right and the infirmary to the left. The dining hall's roof could just be seen down a path between cabins on the opposite side. Right near the center, where all the kids would gather before meals, was the big brass bell used to wake everyone, and call them together.

"I really want to ring that," Nick admitted.

"Me too."

"Think Gillian would mind?"

Gillian was the camp owner and director, a true success story. She'd risen through the ranks, starting as a counsellor like the rest of them and becoming camp director a decade ago. Recently she'd been able to buy the entire thing using family inheritance. She'd been one of their group of tight-knit friends, and the driving force behind this reunion weekend.

"Maybe she would," a voice said from behind, "but one ring wouldn't hurt."

They spun to see a woman a few feet away, wearing jeans and a sweater to hold back the chilly fall breeze. Both had been so entranced that she'd approached without them hearing.

"Gillian!" Nick said and rushed forward.

The two hugged and Patrick followed, doing the same.

The twentyish girl Gillian had been in their days here was still recognizable in the features of the forty-something woman.

After the hug Nick ran over to the bell and gave it one hard ring. The sound reverberated off of the surrounding cabins and trees and mountains, echoing away into nothing.

"I always wondered what the neighbours thought about that bell," Patrick said. "It gets rung pretty early."

Gillian laughed. "Well Camp White Bear has been here almost a hundred years. Anyone buying a property near a kid's camp and expecting peace deserves what they get."

"True."

"Even Luthor?" Nick said, returning to them.

"Luthor?" Patrick cocked his head.

"You know. One of Theo's stories!" Nick explained.

"Oh, yeah. I remember now."

"Anyway," Gillian added, "most of the nearby cottages are empty by this time, now that the nicer weather is all done."

"I remember August nights getting pretty nippy up here."

Gillian shrugged, looked over at the bell. "You want to ring it too, don't you?"

"Well..."

"Go on."

Patrick rushed over ond gave it a ring. This close up the reverberations were hell inside the ear. Some of them had surely ended up with tinnitus from this old brass monster.

"We the first ones?" Nick asked.

"You are."

"Amazing! I call top bunk."

They would all be staying inside one of the junior boy cabins on the upper compound. Inside waited six sets of bunk beds which kids had fought for the right to sleep on top of since long before the days they'd worked here.

"I suspect our friends will be fighting for bottom bunk these days," Patrick said.

"Pftttt," Nick spat. "No sense of adventure."

"Why don't you go claim your beds," Gillian said, pointing toward one particular cabin. "There are fresh sheets and the cabin has been aired out."

"Cool! Come on Pat."

"The bottom bunk with a bag on it is mine," Gillian warned.

Nick laughed, starting toward the cabin. "You're the boss."

Pat started to follow and turned back. "Aren't you coming?"

"Someone should be ready to greet the others."

"Right. Of course."

Pat found a bit of disappointment in that. Now that he'd been reunited with his old friend he didn't want to leave her. Like most of their group they'd stayed in touch over the years. He'd followed her career and her attempts to bring in donations, donating himself since starting to make adult money.

Nick had already reached the cabin and whipped open the door, making Pat rush to catch up. Nick made *hurry up* motions.

"Still no lights in the cabins," Nick observed.

No lights. No power. The only places on camp property that ever had power were the office, the staff lounge, the bathrooms, and the dining hall.

More nostalgia waited inside. The steel-frame beds could have been the same ones from twenty years ago but hopefully with newer mattresses. To the left was a long shelf where kids put their belongings for the couple of week's stay. As Gillian had said one bed had a small suitcase on it. Nick rushed to another bunk and climbed up to lay on it. The open ceiling was within reach and he slapped the rafters with one hand.

"This one is mine."

Patrick laughed. "You remember when that kid went missing and we searched everywhere?"

"Oh yeah, and he was hiding in one of the cabin's rafters. I had the job of running down the mountain toward town. I swear I was halfway there before I got the all clear."

Something to laugh about that hadn't been so funny at the time.

Nick ran one hand along the rafter, feeling the grooves of words carved into wood.

"Camp Nightmare," he muttered. "There's no escape."

"Creepy—" Pat started.

A scream from outside interrupted him, back where they'd left Gillian.

Nick scrambled to get off the bed while Patrick was already out the door.

CHAPTER

TWO

Four new arrivals stood near Gillian at the bell, all in a flurry of activity. Two of the women jumped up and down around Gillian, exchanging hugs. One of them, a blond with long semi-curly hair, screamed again and again.

"That screamer is Jackie," Nick said.

The other woman was shorter, a little over five foot, and less familiar. She matched Jackie for energy though, shoulder-length mousy hair flying with each bounce. All three jumped in a circle while another woman stood nearby, more reserved but clearly wishing she could be part of the excitement. A step or two further was a guy, standing with all of the bags, smiling at the spectacle.

"Theo!" Pat and Nick called at the same time.

The two rushed toward their old friend who barely saw them coming before he was grabbed in two bear hugs.

"What the…?" Theo managed then said with a laugh. "I sure hope I know you guys."

Nick let go and stepped back, Patrick following suit a moment later.

"Holy shit!" Theo said. "Patrick. Nick."

The reserved woman remained apart from either group, looking from one to the other with a self-conscious expression.

"That's not Lisa, is it?" Nick said, stepping toward her.

A smile crept across her face. "It is."

"You look great!" Nick went and gave the hug Lisa so obviously craved but couldn't claim on her own.

In her twenties Lisa had been a bit overweight but since then had leaned into it and packed on many more pounds. Somehow it suited her. She wore the weight well and dressed for her size, standing as if to say this was who she was, take it or leave it. Reserved but not timid. Like Nick she worked with kids, but in Montreal and at her own daycare.

"Who's the ball of energy with Jackie and Gillian?" Nick asked.

The woman in question rushed over and hugged Nick, then Patrick. "You don't recognize me?"

She was five foot and maybe an inch with an infectious smile. Her outstanding feature—now that she had stopped bopping around—was an upturned nose that gave the impression if you got low enough you could see all the way to her brain.

"Abby?" Patrick said.

"That's me."

Abby was incredibly active on social media, always

posting pictures of her kids, her husband, the dog, what she had for lunch, the mini-van, and anything else of semi-importance in her day. The one thing she never posted were pictures of herself.

"You all came together?" Gillian finally asked.

"Yeah, I picked them up before leaving Montreal," Jackie said.

"Wait!" Nick said. "You passed through Millersville then. Is that burger place still there?"

Theo laughed and looked at the girls. "Told you."

"What?" Nick asked.

"I bet them someone would ask."

"I said it would be you," Abby admitted. "And yes, it's still there."

Nick turned to Patrick who was already nodding. "We can make a side trip on the way out."

It was in the opposite direction from the way they would need to go but worth the detour. Nick looked like a kid at Christmas.

"Ooh, I'll join you," Jackie said, then turned to her passengers. "Any objections?"

There were none.

"I stopped for a burger and fries on the way in."

The voice came from behind them rather than toward the parking lot. Lisa jumped and all turned in the direction of this new arrival. Standing there was a skinny redhead, freckles decorating his cheeks.

"Ben?" Lisa said.

A smile and a nod. Lisa rushed forward and gave him a hug, seeming to lose any shyness. Ben had been the youngest of their group, an ex-camper who returned as staff.

"Where did you come from?" Theo asked.

Ben jerked a thumb behind him. "Came up the path. I was looking in on my parents' cottage since I was early."

"That's your car?" Patrick asked. Looking toward the rusted junker next to his rental.

"It is, though car might be generous." He laughed. "More like a collection of rust around a motor."

"Ah, but it's paid for, right," Nick asked. Always the one to find a bright side.

"Well, that is true. It's all mine."

"I forgot your parents have a cottage up here," Lisa said.

"Yeah, they're looking at selling now that they're too old to really enjoy it. I was seeing what repairs are needed."

"You don't want it?" Patrick asked.

"I live in Winnipeg now. Just drove out for the weekend."

A couple sets of eyes turned toward his car.

"It's more reliable than it looks," Ben said.

"Another car coming," Theo said, turning toward the road.

"Who's left?" Abby asked.

Gillian raised a hand, counting off fingers with each name. "Sabrina. Miles. Rob. Erik."

"Erik?" Ben muttered.

"Kind of surprised he's coming myself," Theo said.

Gillian shrugged. "He's turned his life around... or is trying to."

Erik had always been the abrasive one in the group, the one that pushed it with comments and jokes until people had enough and needed to distance themselves. Other than walking away at camp, it was hard to remove yourself from someone. The staff wasn't that large and neither was the property. The only problem was, if you weren't the target of Erik's attention, he could be hilarious. After camp his fractious personality and wild child lifestyle ran him into legal problems. Most of them had no details on all of that.

Ben muttered something to himself again.

A very expensive and obviously new Porshe zoomed into view.

"One of the cottage residents?" Patrick wondered.

The car turned into the parking lot and came to a halt, the well-tuned engine going silent. It sat a moment, the occupant invisible through tinted windows. Nothing moved.

"Are they coming out or what?" Nick asked.

"Change of mind?" Jackie said.

"Gotta be Sabrina," Abby said. "She always knew how to be dramatic."

Sabrina was the one among them that had done very well for herself, and distanced herself most effectively. She was a musical agent living in New York, representing several well-known bands... after a brief and semi-successful attempt at a singing career of her own. She'd made it clear that she wasn't sure if she could get away for this weekend.

The door opened and out stepped a tall, slim woman, dressed in expensive designer jeans, a Hilfiger jacket, and a set of impractical boots which would have been better walking the streets of a city. Her raven-black hair was pulled into a pony-tail. Dark sunglasses hid her eyes.

"Sabrina!" Jackie screamed and broke into a run.

After a brief hesitation Abby joined her. There was a quick reunion of the three halfway to the main group. Jackie and Abby once again jumping up and down with excitement while Sabrina did not. She gave each of them a smile and returned their hugs though. The three returned to the group arm-in-arm.

"Slower car coming behind me," Sabrina said as the others gave her hugs of greeting.

"You came together?" Gillian asked.

"I passed them on the road. They drive like my grandmother."

Abby pulled out a phone as they stood there, mumbling about how she needed to text her kids and husband to let them know she'd arrived.

"Don't bother," Gillian said. "Last place cell phones work is halfway up the mountain."

Abby tapped her screen and confirmed that. She sighed. For the weekend all phones would be very expensive pocket watches.

"You can use the one in the office," Gillian told her.

Abby glanced over at the building, chewing at her lower lip. "It can wait."

Five minutes later another car approached, heard in the distance first before finally coming into view. As it approached the sun went behind one wide cloud, heavy shadows chasing this final arrival along the road. They pulled in behind Sabrina's Porshe and out popped two men from the front seats. The driver was a giant of a man, both is stature and personality. He was already animated and waving at everyone.

"Greetings!" he boomed.

Miles worked construction these days but had run the sports program at camp for several years. The other man, Rob, was small in comparison but still larger than anyone else.

"Miles," Gillian said as they got closer. "Rob."

A third person removed themselves from the back seat, gaze shifting to the road as if unsure that he actually wanted to be here. He came across the open area with no hint of urgency or excitement and arrived amid the hugs and laughs of the others greeting Miles and Rob.

"Hey, everyone," he said.

"Erik," Gillian answered and gave him a hug.

"Good to see you all," he turned to Ben. "Hey Mouse."

Ben turned away, mouth set into a tight line. Erik opened his mouth to say more then gave his head a shake.

"Well, well," Nick observed. "The gang's all here."

Gillian clapped her hands together. "Everyone get your stuff in the cabin. Lunch will be in fifteen minutes."

THREE

Stepping into the dining hall after twenty years was more memories that made everyone's head swim. Like the cabins and the landing, it hadn't changed in any significant way. The same long tables and benches made of solid, heavy wood. The windows had what looked like thirty years of dirty fingerprints all over them, though they were cleaned at the beginning of every summer. Some more recent paint on the walls and a new entry rug, but it still *felt* the same. Two of the tables had been set end to end for them to eat as one big group.

"That smell," Nick muttered.

Nods from several people. The wide open room still held smells of porridge, overcooked toast and shepherd's pie.

"Takes you back, doesn't it?" Gillian said, stepping forward and turning to the group.

Jackie rushed to one long table a bit beyond the entry,

stopping at the chair at its head and running one hand along it. "Three summers I ate meals at this table."

Rob joined her a moment then moved two tables down to do the same. All looked around with a sense of mingled wonder. A return to a simpler time, before bills and mortgages, jobs and spouses. When their entire lives were still ahead of them.

Most milled about the entry, overwhelmed by their own memories.

Miles stared out the window giving a slow shake of his head. The dining hall sat at the top of a slope and gave the best view of the surrounding trees which seemed to go on forever.

"Something wrong?" Pat asked.

"No. It's just... humbling. So much nature," he half laughed. "I mean, there could be *anything* hidden out there."

"Well, don't all stand there," Gillian said. "Come in and look around."

Gillian was always the most enthusiastic about camp life. So much that she never really left, except to get her masters in business. Even now as owner she couldn't be making as much as she could at a regular business. Being here was worth more than that to her.

None of them had returned for a visit in all that time. For many it was as if when their time here was over it was simply time to move on. They kept in touch, through social media, Christmas cards in December, watched each other's successes.

Such as they were.

Theo was still a struggling horror author with middling

success. Abby had married well and become a mother of four, but once that last kid went off to college what would she have? Sabrina was the most successful in terms or career but had no one meaningful in her life. Patrick had crossed the country and made more money in his job than most but knew the kids he'd affected in those five years working here were a greater accomplishment than anything since.

They'd been a small family back then... well, maybe not so small. All of them had been in their last years of high school and into the beginning of university.

"This is Doris," Gillian said, gesturing toward the open door into the kitchen where an older woman stood, wiping hands on an apron. She seemed in her mid-sixties, wearing the sort of smile every grandparent should have. "She's been cook here for eight summers now."

"Hello everyone," Doris said, voice warm and amiable. She raised one hand in greeting, a flash of metal on her finger glinting off the kitchen lights. Unconventional for a wedding ring it held a green stone at the center rather than the usual diamond.

"Her husband Claude is the maintenance man."

"Right here," came a voice from further in the kitchen.

A man came to stand beside Doris. He wore the camouflage clothing of a hunter and had a rifle slung over one shoulder by its strap. He flashed them all a smile and a wave as he passed through.

"Sorry," Doris said. "Claude has to run."

With that Claude was out the door. Jackie gritted her teeth against the idea of hunting. Not that she was a vegetarian or anything, but just the idea of it...

"Please don't hold it against him," Doris said, seeing the expressions. "It's part of the reality up here in the colder months."

Deep breaths. Some nods.

"Always nice to know someone is roaming camp with a gun," Jackie muttered.

"And in camouflage, no less," Erik said in an equally low voice.

In their day the cook had also been a nice older lady but the maintenance man had been a grump who complained about every chore needing to be done. That man had scowled at the kids and looked at staff as if they were making his job harder on purpose.

"Smells great," Lisa said, changing subject and coming closer to the kitchen. "Exactly what I remember."

"Is that..." Nick sniffed the aroma coming from the kitchen. "Shepherd's Pie? I thought I was imagining it."

Gillian laughed. "Not the gourmet feast you all deserve but I thought this somehow more fitting."

Patrick's stomach rumbled in anticipation. He hadn't eaten shepherd's pie in decades, couldn't look at the stuff for years after working here, but right now it seemed like a delicacy.

Sabrina sniffed and looked away from the kitchen doors.

"Not looking forward to shepherd's pie?" Patrick asked in a low voice only Sabrina could have heard.

It was as if a switch were flipped. Her scowl became a smile and she shrugged, more in the moment. "It was never my favorite but it will do, I suppose."

Patrick laughed, wondering if it was actually anyone's favorite meal.

Potatoes, meat and corn made it a quick and easy meal to feed a large group of children, and most important it was cheap. Camp White Bear was for kids from low-income houses, severely broken homes, and foster care. Every year it struggled to get the necessary donations to keep going. Government grants helped and what little the parents could afford to pay filled in some of the shortfall.

"Hope you've got ketchup," Rob said.

Dry sarcastic wit had always been his skill, something probably not in much demand during his day job as an admin with the federal government.

"Amen to that," Ben agreed.

They sat around the joined tables envisioning how as counsellors they'd sat three kids on each side with an adult on one end and another lucky kid opposite.

Gillian remained standing at an empty chair, mid way along the table.

"You gonna give us a speech?" Nick asked.

"Oh, please do," Sabrina added.

It was hard to tell if that was sarcasm.

"I... Okay," Gillian nodded. "I just wanted to say, you are all my heroes."

No response to that. Some glanced self-consciously at their neighbour. A shrug here and there.

"What do you mean?" Abby asked.

Gillian took a deep breath. "You all came here, gave your summers to work in a job that paid less than working at McDonalds. You made a difference in the lives of about seven hundred kids every summer. A bunch of kids that didn't have much positive stuff in their lives otherwise."

"Aw, Gillian," Miles said.

"Whatever else you've done in your lives your time here balances it all out. You've made a difference."

A quick glance at Erik who managed to keep eye contact then silence rushed in as Gillian finished and looked down at the table.

Miles cleared his throat. Nick sat back in his seat and Patrick took a deep breath.

"You're the hero, Gillian," Lisa said in a low voice.

Nick nodded. "Absolutely."

Gillian shook her head but Lisa continued. "You stayed here while the rest of us moved on. You made this your life and done wonders with keeping camp going."

"You put your own money into it too," Theo added. "Bought the place."

Gillian took her seat. "Thank you. All of you."

More silence.

"Way to kill the party vibe, Gillian," Erik said.

She laughed and the awkwardness was broken. Everyone joined in, laughing a bit harder than the joke truly deserved. Ben smiled and looked anywhere but at Erik.

"Anyone remember," Nick asked, leaning forward against the table. "Theo's story about the crazy cook?"

Theo laughed and Gillian groaned just as Doris brought the first tray of shepherd's pie to the table and placed it before them.

"As I recall her name was Doris too," Gillian said.

All turned to the woman standing before them who

winked. "Don't tell Gillian, but the hamburger is actually slow camper."

They all howled with laughter.

"That's right!" Miles said, pounding the table with one open palm. "The crazy cook grabbed the slowest one in line."

"How did you know?" Theo asked Doris.

The cook glanced at Gillian then back again. "My kids were campers here when you were all counsellors."

"Uh-oh," Theo said. "Your last name isn't Voorhees, is it?"

Doris laughed. "No, and my kids had a great time. No one drowned."

She turned and headed back to the kitchen for the next tray or food.

"Oh, I like her," Jackie said to Gillian.

The friends served themselves. Rob grabbed the ketchup, as if afraid there would not be enough to go around.

"The story I remember most," Lisa said, "is the axe-man who lived in the woods."

"Yes! Luthor," Rob added. "Each year he would come and take one person from a cabin in the middle of the night."

"He hated the sound of the bell."

"My favorite were the doppelgangers," Patrick said. "The creatures who would replace someone."

Abby looked thoughtful. "Didn't Theo convince your entire cabin that you'd been replaced by one of those creatures?"

"Yes, he did and that was fun," Patrick laughed. "I woke up to the whole cabin shining their flashlights in my face to see if it shifted. Thanks for that Theo."

Theo leaned back with a reminiscing smile. "Because a Doppelganger couldn't keep pretending for long without shifting, right? I'd forgotten that one."

The kids and staff had been his most receptive audience and what really refined his story telling skills. In those days the stories were real, believed. He was able to play around with them and if one didn't work, he could abandon it and move on to the next.

"You know, it was really inappropriate to tell those stories to six and seven year olds," Gillian said, half serious. "I'd fire someone for that these days."

"It was twenty years ago," Theo raised both hands in defence. "A different time… and the statute of limitations has expired for punishing me."

Gillian laughed again.

"Besides, I didn't tell them to the younger kids… well, not as often anyway."

"I liked your daytime stories better," Gillian said.

"What? The Fluffies?" Theo said. "King Raccoon? Seriously?"

"Absolutely. You should do a book of those."

"The shadows!" Miles half yelled, dragging the conversation back. "I was terrified to go to the bathroom after hours for that entire summer."

"I should write these down," Theo said. "Some forgotten treasures here."

"Hmph," Gillian snorted. "As I recall the old crazy cook made the slowest kid into hamburgers, not shepherd's pie."

"Depended what was for dinner that night," Theo admitted. "I adapted."

"Oh!" Patrick added, remembering a detail. "Didn't the axe-man have a cabin nearby, just past the camping sites?"

"Don't forget the Wendigo," Abby added. "It came from an ancient burial ground nearby."

"Cultural misappropriation at its best," Sabrina sniffed.

"Guilty as charged," Theo admitted. "And I wouldn't touch anything indigenous these days. Too bad because there are some great stories."

"That one made no sense though," Sabrina argued. "Why would a wendigo come from a graveyard. It isn't a ghost. It's a creature that stalks people through the woods."

Theo shrugged. "You seem to know a lot about it."

"I took a course in college on indigenous folklore."

"Ah, that explains it. You're right, it made absolutely no sense. The wendigo is also a hunger spirit, tied to cannibalism."

"Yuck," she shot back.

"The Crying Boy," Erik said. "Remember him?"

"That story freaked me out," Ben said.

"Everything freaked you out Mouse," Erik said.

Ben was silent a moment, not looking at Erik. "I always hated that nickname."

"Yeah, but you were small and timid," Erik said. "It fit."

Ben said nothing.

"Are you still that timid?" Erik added, needling their friend.

"N... N... No."

"Still got that stutter," Erik teased.

"Leave me alone y... y... you, thug."

"Thug?" Erik said, mock offended.

"Erik!" Lisa cautioned. "Don't make fun of him."

"Ah, Lisa to the rescue," Erik mused. "Some things never change."

"L... L... leave her alone!" Ben jumped to his feet, fists clenched.

"Whoa, guys," Patrick said. "We're all friends here."

It had obviously been a bad idea letting Erik sit near Ben, not that they could have been separated that much. Erik had always been a pain in the ass, and poor, quiet Ben was his target of choice because he could get a rise so easily.

"Relax Mouse."

"Don't call me that!" Ben slammed his hand down on the table, just catching the edge of his plate, throwing half-finished shepherd's pie all over himself. "God damn it!"

Ben stood, a deep flush of red filling his face. He stood a moment looking at the mess he'd made, glancing at each of his old friends, some of which made no eye contact while others showed back pity.

"Fuck!" Ben stormed for the dining hall door and out into the sunshine.

Silence filled the room until Erik let out a disbelieving laugh.

"Some things never change, do they?" Gillian shot back.

"Oh, come on, it was a joke."

Gillian shook her head and returned to her food. Erik glanced around at the rest, none of which would meet his eyes.

"Seriously? All of you? Did anyone keep their sense of humour?"

Back in the day Patrick, Nick and Theo all found Erik's

antics hilarious and encouraged him with their laughs, even when aimed at them.

But now...

"Okay, okay, I get the message," Erik sighed, getting to his feet. "I'll go chat with the little runt."

"Erik!"

"Relax, Gillian. I don't plan on leading with calling him a runt."

Erik slipped out the door, allowing the spring to slam it behind him. Hopefully Erik would find Ben quickly and smooth things over. He could be a pain but he also could turn on the charm when he wanted. In the meantime, the rest continued to eat and chat about Theo's stories from back then.

Twenty minutes later Erik returned with a shrug, the dining hall door banging shut again. "Couldn't find him."

"Did you check the cabin?" Lisa asked.

"You mean the single most obvious location? Must have forgotten that one." He rolled his eyes. "I checked there, the upper compound, the road, the staff hall. Nice new furniture in there, by the way. I even went down to the pool."

"Maybe he headed to his parent's cottage," Jackie suggested.

Erik groaned. "You're all going to make me hunt him down, aren't you?"

No response. Gillian and Lisa's glare burned into Erik.

"Fine, anyone remember where the cottage is?"

A glance around at a bunch of empty expressions.

"No? Well, that solves that. Guess we wait for the Mouse to return on his own. Shall I put out some cheese?"

Patrick and Theo both laughed.

"While we wait." Erik turned to Theo. "Tell us one of your stories from back then."

"Aw, I don't know."

"Yeah, come on, Theo," Nick added. "You'll never have a more captive audience."

"Can't argue with that."

Interlude 1 – 20 Years Ago – The Shadows

THE KIDS SAT in a tight group, waiting for Theo's story. This wasn't the first time he'd come to tell a story to Patrick and Nick's combined cabins. These were the older boys and they knew what to expect. They looked forward to it.

"Years ago…"

No! Theo chastised himself. The last time he told them a story it had been *years ago*. They can't all be years ago… Or could they? Didn't matter now, he was committed.

"Years ago, when this camp was brand new and no one knew what lived in these mountains, the first campers came here."

Jaspal leaned forward, already drawn in. There was a kid who loved horror stories.

"A young boy… just your age actually… woke up in the middle of the night. He had to pee."

A couple of giggles. They all knew what that was like.

"This boy, Neville, *always* had to pee at night."

"Just like Heath," one kid at the back said.

"Shut up!" Heath shot back.

Theo waited, patient.

Jaspal never looked back to Theo. "What happened to Neville?"

"The first couple of nights? Nothing. His counsellor would get up and take him to the bathroom, but that got annoying quick. His counsellor just wanted to sleep, you know? He told Neville to wake one of the other boys."

"Did he?"

"Yep, for a while. Then his friends got tired of taking turns. They all told him to go by himself."

"You can't do that," Heath said. "We can't go alone."

"Oh, I know," Theo said. "I know. But when you gotta go, you gotta go."

Heath settled back, understanding the conflict perfectly.

"So, Neville went to the bathroom by himself for the first time. At night, alone, Camp looks like a different place. The shadows are deeper, like they can just suck you in."

"Camp Nightmare," Heath whispered to Jaspal.

Jaspal chuckled.

Good for you Heath.

Now, where was I going?

Oh, the shadows. Yeah.

"As Neville walked to the bathroom he heard a voice."

"What did it say?" Jaspal asked.

"It said: *Come here.*"

"Who said it?"

"Neville couldn't tell. It came from the shadows and he was a smart boy so he didn't stick around. Neville rushed to the bathroom and turned on the lights then did what he went there to do and rushed back to bed. His heart was pounding and his breath was fast, like when you play a long game of soccer."

Some murmurs from the group. Everyone understood running around.

"The next night, Neville had to go again, of course. He had to go every night, and he remembered the sound of that voice. No one would go with him so he held it as long as he could. He held it until it was almost too late. In the end he left the cabin and started for the bathroom. *Come closer.* The voice said. *Come here.*"

"Did he?" Heath asked.

"No, no. Like I said, Neville was a smart boy. Like you. He stayed on the path, stayed in the light from the lamp posts."

Heath breathed a sigh of relief.

"But as he went a light behind him flickered... flickered... went out."

"No," Heath breathed.

"Oh, yes. But that was a problem for the return trip. Neville went to the bathroom, did what he had to do and then started back. He came to that dead, dark, area. You know the one, just beside the park?"

Lots of nods. They knew that light.

"It was between him and his cabin."

"What did he do?" Jaspal asked.

"What could he do? To go another way, he would have to make a full circle, past the dining hall, up and around the bell, past the office. So, he went through the dark spot. Neville stood in the darkness, the shadows around him rushing closer with the absence of that light."

All the boys had leaned closer. Heath had both hands up against his cheeks, looking like the kid from Home Alone, but a scarier version, more like that Scream painting. Jaspal's grin stretched from one side of his face to the other.

"*Come closer.* The shadows whispered. *Come here.* Neville felt a burning cold touch on his shoulder, and heard the ragged whisper from right next to his ear."

Eyes were wide. Some kids held their breath.

"Gotcha!" Theo yelled.

Every boy jumped. Patrick and Nick on the other side of the room jumped.

Nervous laughs to cover up their fright.

"What happened to Neville?" Jaspal asked.

"No one knows. When they woke up the next morning he was gone."

"Gone?" Heath said, with a gulp.

"Yep. But that night, there was one more shadow, just outside the bathroom, saying *come closer* in a voice just like Neville's.

CHAPTER
FOUR

Dinnertime brought smells of spaghetti sauce and garlic bread rushing at them as they re-entered the dining hall. More staples from the camp days. There was some debate on whether tomorrow's breakfast would be pancakes or French toast. There was a consensus that no one was hoping for porridge.

"Aw, man," Nick moaned, drawing in a deep sniff of the air. "The nostalgia is killing me."

Gillian laughed, looking through the opening into the kitchen. The counter held all the food ready for the taking. "Doris?"

No response.

She turned back to the others. "Must have gone back to their house."

"She's done the hard part," Miles said. "I'm sure we can handle the rest."

"I'll get plates and utensils," Abby said.

"Need a hand?" Theo followed her through the swinging doors to the kitchen.

Jackie turned to Gillian and raised an eyebrow, receiving a shrug and wry smile in response. Abby and Theo had been *the* couple all those years ago, spanning a couple of summers. But Abby was now a mom with four kids and a successful husband, and Theo had a wife of his own back home.

Nick walked up to the counter and grabbed the big bowl of sauce, ladle half sunk in. "Don't just stand there, someone grab the pasta."

Rob rushed over and got the twin of Nick's bowl filled with long spaghetti noodles and a pair of tongs. Lisa brought the garlic bread. Others found cups and drinks and brought those to the table. Soon they were all sitting and eating.

"Still no Ben?" Lisa asked, glancing toward the door as if saying his name might conjure their missing friend.

No such luck.

Erik groaned. "I took a walk and looked at some of the nearby cabins for signs of life but didn't see anything. They all look to be shut up for winter."

"Is his parent's cottage further away?" Nick asked.

Shrugs from all around.

"Has anyone ever been there?"

"I have," Rob said. "Came up here once in the fall, after camp."

Erik threw up his hands. "That would have been useful info before I went looking."

"It was two decades ago. I don't even remember what the outside looked like."

"You hung out with Ben?" Patrick asked.

"For a bit," Rob admitted around a mouthful of garlic bread. "But we drifted apart without this place in common."

"I get that." Erik grunted and fell silent.

"Well, we know Erik went looking at cottage this afternoon," Gillian said. "What about the rest of you?"

"Most of us went down to the lake," Patrick said. "Went swimming."

"In this temperature?" Gillian said.

"Too cold for my taste," Miles agreed. "I looked around the cabins and stuff. Went down to the sports field."

"Anyone go to the old creepy graveyard?" Theo asked.

Shakes of the head all around.

"Did you?" Rob asked.

"Hell no. I like to tell the stories, not be part of one."

Everyone laughed.

"It's not haunted." Gillian rolled her eyes.

"Says you," Theo shot back. "It was spooky as hell back in the day."

"Yeah, and we always went at night," Jackie said. "No wonder we have creepy memories."

They all continued the meal, enjoying each other's company, remembering how to talk to each other.

"Stupid question," Patrick said, "but has anyone noticed if Ben's car is still there?"

Blank stares all around, embarrassed glances.

Nope. Not one of them.

"Erik?"

"I didn't even know he had a car."

Patrick nodded. "Yeah, fair."

"Didn't someone park behind him?" Gillian asked. "It was the rusty car."

No one could remember who parked where.

Patrick hesitated a moment then pushed back from the table, his dinner mostly finished anyway. There was a sudden desire to just get outside, to see the sky and experience the smells of camp as sunset approached.

"I'll go check."

"Hold up," Nick said, getting to his feet as well, though his dinner was less complete. "I'll come with you."

Patrick waited at the door while Nick made his way across the room and the two passed into the chillier air of approaching evening. The sun was still above the horizon and would be for another half hour or so but night fell hard here.

"You didn't have to come," Pat said.

"It'll only take a minute," Nick answered as they walked. "Either it's there or it isn't."

Patrick nodded. "And if it isn't?"

"Well... then either Ben had enough of Erik and just left, or he did go to his parent's cabin."

"Then our next step would be...?"

Nick laughed aloud realizing what Pat was up to. This was one of the logic games they would do on car rides across the border into Plattsburgh or Burlington all those years ago. Something neither realized how much they missed until this moment. The two of them had been in the same high school and come here together to work. Theirs was one friendship which had lasted, even though half the country separated them.

"Well," Nick answered after a moment's thought. "If he's gone to the cabin then a stroll up a few roads here should eventually find him."

"Elementary, my dear Nicholas."

"Watson ejaculated."

Patrick snorted out a laugh at that. They'd both shared a love of Sherlock Holmes but some of the word choices were unfortunate and hilarious. So many times, there would be a dialogue tag of *Watson Ejaculated*. As teens this was endlessly hilarious.

"You know, Nick, a weight has lifted from me since getting here."

"I know what you mean. For a little while I can almost pretend I'm that kid from all those years ago. No responsibilities. No bills. No job. No mortgage."

"Glory days."

"Yeah, I—"

Patrick stumbled to a halt. "What the hell?"

Nick looked up. "What is it?"

Patrick pointed toward where the small parking lot should have been. Now it and their cars, plus the road beyond were gone, replaced by trees as far as the eye could see. It was as if there'd never been a road at all.

FIVE

The two old friends stared at the spot for several seconds, brains struggling to absorb what their eyes saw. Nick took one step toward the spot where the cars had been parked then stopped.

"Where...? What...?"

Patrick shook his head. "Impossible."

Impossible or not it seemed true. Patrick spun in a circle, going on the theory that they had somehow gotten turned around and were facing the wrong way, or that they had turned right coming out of the dining hall instead of left. Except... the office was on their left and the infirmary on the right. The road should have run behind the two.

The trees were tall, at least the height of a four-storey building. Gnarled limbs pointed from the main trunk, speaking of their age. On one tree a branch closer to the ground had been broken some time ago and still hung from splinters of wood. The coloring inside was aged and weathered.

"The cars are gone," Nick said needlessly.

"Replaced by trees a hundred years old."

"A hundred...? Pat there was a road there this morning, and a parking lot."

"I remember."

"Well, both can't be true."

"Agreed."

"So, could... Could someone have planted...?" Nick ran down, realizing just how stupid it sounded.

It would have taken a crew of dozens to transplant and erect one tree this size much less the forest that now spread before them. Even if some mad group of arborists had managed this, they wouldn't have been able to do it without notice. Someone would have seen this happen.

Nick looked at his watch. "It's only been like six hours since we arrived."

Patrick nodded, understanding Nick's point. There just wasn't enough time to complete an undertaking this massive.

Skin prickling, the little part of his lizard brain that told him to just run yammering in overdrive, Patrick stepped forward.

"You sure you want to get closer?" Nick said.

"Not really."

"I don't like this."

Patrick huffed out a breath. "Me either."

"So lets—"

"I just want to see the earth around one tree."

"Why?"

Instead of answering Patrick shuffled forward to crouch at the base of the closest tree. He ran his hands through the dirt there. "Hard packed soil. The roots are deep. These trees have been here a very long time."

"Impossible!"

"What's the quote?" Patrick asked. "When you have eliminated the impossible, whatever is left, however improbable—"

"Yeah, but all we have is the impossible."

"Time travel?"

"You mean we've all jumped back a hundred years? The camp included."

"We were talking about the impossible."

"Let's add aliens and magic to the list of suspects."

A flicker of shadows deeper into the trees had Patrick back on his feet and retreating.

"What is it?" Nick asked.

"I thought I saw something move."

Nick stared into the trees, glancing left and right. "Raccoon maybe?"

"They don't come out this early."

"Yeah, 'cause that would be the most ridiculous thing to happen tonight."

"Ben?" Pat called.

Nick glanced to him then back again, joining the call.

No further movement.

No nothing.

"You hear that?" Pat asked.

"What?"

"Silence. No birdsong. No insects."

Nothing at all.

"Let's go tell the others."

The two started back toward the dining hall, glancing over their shoulders as they went.

SIX

"Bullshit," Erik said.

Lisa shook her head. "I don't get the joke."

Nick threw his hands up, voice rising. "It's no joke."

Patrick placed a hand on his friend's shoulder. "I wouldn't believe it either, would you?"

Nick let out a long, frustrated breath. "Fine! We'll show you."

"I'm not walking to the upper compound just so you can laugh about tricking me," Erik said.

"Whatever." Nick turned for the door. "Stay here then."

Patrick came up beside him and the two glanced back. The rest looked to each other, waiting for someone to make the decision to follow. Rob gave a shrug and fell in with them. Gillian joined a moment later. After that everyone seemed to decide it was okay to go since they were not the first ones tricked. They were just coming along to see how gullible Rob and Gillian were. The last person to join was Erik, arms crossed in protest.

The group was mostly silent on the short walk, no one really certain how to react. Was it simply an obvious joke? Or were Nick and Patrick trying for something else? Gillian walked next to the two, almost leading the way, Rob a step behind.

"Just to be clear," Jackie said from somewhere in the middle, "we all know this is a lame joke, right? I mean, trees don't just grow up to obscure a road.

Obviously.

Everyone knew that.

Only, that's exactly what *had* happened.

The group spread to a wide line, giving everyone a chance to see with their own eyes.

Gillian finally broke the silence, staring into the trees. "This is impossible."

"Pretty much what we said," Nick agreed.

"Where the fuck is my Porshe?" Sabrina spat.

Everyone ignored the outburst. Jackie stepped forward the way Patrick had minutes earlier and examined the earth around one tree. They kept quiet and let her come to her own conclusion.

"These trees are old."

"Oh, come on!" Erik exploded and stomped forward to join Jackie. "This is just some kind of stupid joke. I'll prove it."

He passed Jackie, stumbling over roots and forging his way deeper into what was the start of a thick forest. Jackie rose from her inspection of the tree and started to follow.

"Guys..." Gillian cautioned.

Erik waved one dismissive hand and continued on, or tried to at least. The terrain was uneven and both he and Jackie stumbled over roots and overgrown brush. Passing the second tree into their attempted exploration Erik went down, rolling up against the next tree.

"God damn it!"

"You okay?" Jackie asked.

Using the tree for support he got back to his feet and returned to the others. He passed Jackie—who had given up when Erik wiped out—without a comment.

"Still think it's bullshit?" Nick asked.

Erik's mouth worked, like he was trying to chew something unpleasant. He looked aside, giving all the acknowledgement anyone was likely to get.

"The road is just gone," Jackie said.

"What the hell is going on?" Abby demanded.

"A good question." Sabrina crossed her arms.

All of them turned to Gillian who held her hands up in surrender. "Sorry all, I don't know any more about this than you do."

"You're the one who dragged us all up here," Erik said.

"Dragged? But, you... Well, I mean..." She gestured at the trees. "You think I could do something like *this*?"

"I've been doing construction since our camp days," Miles said, staring at the trees, "and I don't think anyone could do something like this. Not in the time available, and certainly not without us noticing."

A few nods of agreement, though none had the same expertise.

"So…" Lisa said, voice low and uncertain. "What do we do?"

"We gotta get out of here," Erik said.

Sabrina shook her head still staring at the spot her car had occupied hours earlier. "Why the hell did I ever come back here?"

"Old friends?" Patrick suggested.

"The ability to lord your success over others," Abby muttered a little too loud.

Sabrina glared at her a second before turning on Patrick. "Friends? Wonderful. Now I'm trapped with all my *friends*."

Trapped.

A word that everyone had at the front of their mind, trying to push aside. One word that none of them had mentioned aloud but now that it was out the reality rocked them all. They *were* trapped. The surrounding wilderness had pressed in on them and wasn't about to let them go it seemed.

Gillian turned to the trees and back again. "Okay, nothing bad has happened—"

"Yet," Erik added, with a glare from Gillian.

"I have to get out of here," Abby said suddenly. "I have to get back to my kids."

The tears were close.

The panic was closer.

She pulled out her phone at the same time as Sabrina, both knowing it was hopeless. There was no service here and there hadn't been before anything weird happened.

"I have to go," Abby repeated, half begging, eyes on her useless phone.

"Relax, Abby," Patrick said in a calm, low voice. "We'll be okay."

She rounded on him. "Will we? Are you sure about that? We are *trapped* here. The trees have closed in on us, Patrick. The *trees!* The road is just gone and so are our cars. How will we be okay?"

He stepped back under the frenzied insistence of Abby's tirade.

"I... Well..." He found he had no answer that didn't sound lame and dismissive.

Rob said. "The sun is still setting."

Everyone turned to the west and the sun which was lower in the sky. They had another half hour to forty-five minutes before the darkness of night would completely embrace them.

What then?

"The landline!" Gillian said with a snap of her fingers.

Abby looked at her. "The what?"

"The phone. In the office."

Abby's face brightened.

"And who do we call?" Erik asked.

"The police—" Abby started.

"Uh-huh," Erik continued. "Hello officer, we're at Camp *Nightmare* and the trees have closed in on us. I'm seeing it with my own eyes and not believing it."

Abby's face crumpled under the weight of Erik's logic.

"Easy Erik," Miles said. "We're all in this together."

Erik snorted out a half laugh and rolled his eyes, but he said no more.

"I have some friends in town," Gillian said. "I'll call one of them."

"And tell them what?" Abby said in a fragile voice.

"I don't know. Maybe just that I need their help."

"Tell them to bring chainsaws," Rob said.

"How far down the mountain does that forest go?" Abby asked. "Is there any road left?"

Gillian put an arm around Abby's shoulders. "Let's just make some calls before we panic, okay?"

"What are we waiting for?" Erik demanded.

The physical contact seemed to help Abby. She nodded acceptance and allowed Gillian to guide her toward the office. The others followed, accepting this tie to civilization as a potential solution. True the town was at least thirty minutes away, down the winding road that led out of the small mountain. It was something though. Gillian climbed the office steps first, Abby just behind, and passed through the door. Inside was a room none of them had spent much time in while working here, where the business side of camp was done. Even the camp director spent as little time as needed inside. Better to be out and about on beautiful days. The small reception type area held an empty desk and no phone. Children's pictures of King Raccoon and the fluffies littered the walls at various heights. Gillian kept going though an open doorway and down the following hall up to another office, hers. The friends crowded in while Gillian rushed across to the desk and grabbed an old-time phone with an actual rotary dial, heavy enough to use as a weapon if it came to it. Pressing the receiver to her ear she had one finger poised to dial then stopped. Her eyes darted to them then back to the phone as her finger pressed on the connector where the receiver had sat.

CLICK! CLICK! CLICK! CLICK!

The hand holding the receiver dropped to her side.

"Let me guess," Erik said. "Dead."

She nodded, eyes darting back and forth as if another solution would jump out at them. The eleven friends pressed in close together in a room that would have been crowded with six. They looked from face to face, hoping someone had an idea of what to do next. Patrick leaned against the wall next to the door, bumping a framed picture. He grabbed it to stop the whole thing from crashing to the floor.

"What..." Abby gasped trying to hold back tears. "What...?"

Rob placed a hand on her shoulder. "It's—"

"Don't touch me!"

He jerked back like he'd accidentally touched the hot burner on a stove.

Abby turned on Gillian. "You're in charge here. You brought us here. What do we do?"

"Well..." Gillian replaced the receiver on the phone. "We could..."

Abby sagged into the chair in front of Gillian's desk, head in her hands, muttering. "I knew I should have called the kids earlier."

"The staff lounge," Sabrina said. "Is there still a phone down there?"

Gillian nodded.

In the summer time when there were a bunch of teens and twenty-something staff members on site it was the only way to reach family back in Montreal or Ottawa. Back then anyway. Today everyone would have a cell phone though apparently it would take a walk down the mountain to find any service.

"Yeah," Erik said. "We go down there and waste time discovering that phone doesn't work either."

"What do you suggest then?" Gillian's frustration clear in her voice.

"Me? I..." He thought for a moment. "Okay, there was a path, down past the pool and into the woods."

"Where the campsites are?" Theo asked.

"Yeah, exactly. If you keep going past the campsites there's a way out to the road further down."

Rob looked dubious. "And you want to follow this instead of checking the other phone?"

"Yeah, I do. Before it gets too dark to be an option."

A couple of them looked in the proposed direction. No one offered to join Erik and he shook his head.

"What is the matter with all of you? You're back to being the kids you were when we worked here. Following the camp director. Letting others make decisions for you."

Patrick shrugged. "What are you—?"

"Wake up, Patrick! This isn't natural," Erik gestured toward the missing road, turning to each of them. "This isn't a practical joke. This isn't some mistake that will solve itself."

He glanced at Gillian.

"I'm as trapped as you are." She raised both hands defensively.

"Yeah, so do we wait and see who… or what has trapped us here?"

Abby shivered against the idea of a *what* that might be trapping them. Her mind was overwhelmed, shutting down and she allowed her attention to be drawn to the mess which was Gillian's desk top. It was a pile of papers, pens, scissors, tape, a few rocks, a screwdriver and other objects that should have been put away long ago. It seemed like the land of the forgotten, where things went to die. Rolled up against the base of the lamp was a small metal cylinder. She reached out absently with one finger and rolled the object toward her, pinching it between two fingers. A bullet? Small caliber and—

"I'm going to try for that road." Erik said.

"What?" Gillian exploded. "Why? This is just a… a…"

"Just what, Gillian?" Erik asked.

She shrugged. No answer available.

"What do *you* think is going on here, Erik?" Patrick asked.

"Me? No idea. Something supernatural."

"I was thinking time travel," Miles said.

"Time travel?" Sabrina scoffed.

Miles shrugged. "It would explain the trees."

"Magic would explain it too," Theo said.

Silence rushed in as each thought their own theories.

Jackie half raised one hand. "I'll come with you, Erik."

No one else volunteered to head into the woods in the growing darkness with them.

Erik shrugged. "When I have cell service I'll call 911 for help, but I ain't coming back."

"What will you tell them?" Abby asked in a quiet voice, one hand gripped into a fist.

"I don't know. Maybe that there's a fire. That gets people moving."

"Wait!" Gillian said. "If you're insisting on doing this then take flashlights. There are a bunch in the entry. I got enough for everyone and…" She trailed off, unsure of what else to say. She'd gotten them knowing most wouldn't even consider bringing one. She opened a desk drawer and pulled out one of her own.

"It *will* be dark soon," she finally added.

Erik and Jackie headed for the entry, the others following, each wondering if they shouldn't just follow the duo into the woods. Everyone grabbed one of the waiting flashlights, all lined up side by side on a shelf. The front door slammed closed a moment later as Erik and Jackie crossed the upper compound, headed down the path toward the pool and beyond.

SEVEN

The remaining friends stepped outside and descended the steps to stand in a quiet cluster, looking around as if something might rush out of the growing dusk. On the opposite side of the upper compound Erik and Jackie disappeared between two cabins. Everyone clutched their flashlights, like someone bobbing in the ocean would grasp a life preserver. Miles clicked his on and off, swishing the beam around for distance. A moment later eight flashlights clicked on—all but Gillian's-- confirming their batteries were fresh and the beam strong enough to light up any area once darkness fully came.

Mostly they all tried to convince themselves they hadn't landed in a nightmare, that there had to be some logical reason for all of it. A logical reason why the phone was dead. A logical reason why trees had suddenly grown up to block them in. A logical reason why both the road and their cars had all disappeared.

The phone by itself wouldn't be so sinister, but add in the rest and it was asking too much of their imaginations. If there was no logical reason though, what was it about? They'd been trapped but nothing had threatened them, or as Erik had pointed out: not yet.

Night was yet to come.

"They should have waited," Gillian huffed out starting for the staff lounge. She glanced at the spot where Erik and Jackie had gone from view. "The phone in the staff lounge will work."

Gillian was trying more to fill the void of silence with a bunch of chatter rather than give any factual information, or she was simply trying to settle her own nerves. If someone had asked which it was, she wouldn't have known herself. No amount of talk was going to solve the mystery of those trees and she knew it.

"It has to work," she added in a low voice to herself,

Patrick placed a hand on her shoulder. He leaned in and said equally low. "This isn't your fault."

"I brought you all here, didn't I?"

"That's true. You probably should have had some contingency plan in case trees sprouted up trapping us here."

"I... Yeah, okay. When you put it like that."

"You invited us for a reunion and we all came. Might as well blame us for showing up."

"I agree with Pat," Theo said from close behind, making the two jump. "Sorry, I wasn't trying to eavesdrop."

"You two aren't as quiet as you think," Lisa added. "And I don't blame you either."

"I do," Sabrina said.

They turned to the taller woman. Sabrina never was able to make a good joke. It always came off sounding harsh and bitchy and she'd long ago given up trying. Right now the expression on her face said she wasn't joking at all.

"This is your fault." Sabrina's hands were clenched fists at her side.

"Be fair," Lisa said.

"I am. This is her camp and she brought us here. Now there are trees trapping us. That's the worst thing that has happened so far." Her eyes shifted toward the trees on the words *so far*. "Something worse is coming."

"You don't know that," Gillian answered.

"No? You think this is all to encourage us to *Kumbaya* around the camp fire?"

"Well—"

"Bad. Things. Are, Coming." Sabrina repeated focussing on Gillian. "And *you* brought us here."

Abby shivered. "Why have we slowed down then? Move!"

They continued toward the long shack which functioned as a staff lounge, a place where the counsellors could get away from the kids in what was at times a twenty-four hour job. The building had a door at either end and another on the long side facing them. Inside was a wide open room with a variety of mismatched couches and chairs that had been donated over the years since they'd been there. It smelled faintly of mustiness and decades worth of cigarette smoke. To one side was a separate room for the phone, allowing a bit of privacy for anyone wanting to call home. The door was closed.

"I will check this time," Sabrina said.

"Be my guest." Gillian ground her jaw then added in a lower voice which could still be heard clearly. "Let it be your fault if it doesn't work."

Sabrina glared over one shoulder then reached for the knob, practically throwing the door into the phone room. It slammed against the inside wall like a bomb in the quiet evening air. One step in Sabrina turned and resumed her glare.

"What the fuck is going on here, Gillian?"

Everyone froze under Sabrina's fury.

"What?" Gillian asked, one hand to her mouth. "What is it?"

Sabrina just gestured, teeth clamped tight, unable or unwilling to speak. Patrick and Rob both squeezed past, followed soon by the others as Sabrina was pushed aside.

"No!" Abby half-wailed. "No, no, no!"

All that remained of the phone were shards of metal and plastic littering the floor. Wires dangled from a hole in the wall.

Miles booted one piece of metal. "It's like someone strapped some explosives to it."

CHAPTER

EIGHT

Sabrina stamped across the small space, the threat of violence plain in her movements. She stopped a foot from Gillian and repeated her last words, practically spitting them into Gillian's face. "What. The fuck. Is going on?"

Gillian retreated a step, hands up, eyes darting to either side for help or escape.

"I... I... I..." She dropped her hands, eyes on the floor, unable to meet anyone's face. "I don't know."

"Well, that's just fucking great," Sabrina threw up her hands.

"No one has been hurt," Gillian added lamely.

"Not that we know of," Rob responded. "We haven't seen Ben since lunch."

"And now Erik and Jackie are out there," Nick added.

Miles muttered in a low voice, "Wonder if it's too late to catch up."

"Let's not panic." Patrick held his hands up for calm.

"Panic?" Abby demanded. "I'm beyond that."

Patrick ignored her. "Gillian, you know this place better than us. What are our options?"

"Options? I... I don't know. No, wait!"

Several people refocussed attention on the camp director, ready for any shred of hope to grasp.

"The old radio is in storage, the one we used for emergency communication, remember?"

Nods from a few as the memory came back. The radio sat in the front office, in one corner out of the way. They used it to communicate with the small towns dotting the country near the bottom of the mountain, and for the walkie-talkies staff took when going to more remote spots, like the boating site by the lake, or the campgrounds.

"What do you want to bet that will be smashed too?" Sabrina said. "Or just completely gone."

Gillian had enough of this negative woman she'd barely tolerated as a girl. The only reason she'd ever been part of their group was because Miles briefly dated her.

"If you have a better suggestion then speak up? Or is your only skill standing there being negative?"

Sabrina glared a moment then chewed on her lip. "Maybe I do. What about the maintenance man's home? Clem?"

"Claude," Gillian corrected.

"Whatever. Maybe he has a working phone."

"*Maybe* he has a working gun." Theo added.

"Yes," Sabrina agreed, annoyed with herself for having

missed this one piece of data. "He was going hunting. He must have something."

That resonated with a few of them.

"If he returned home," Miles said. "If not then one of these cottages might."

"Okay, good." Gillian threw out her hands in a request to stop. "Which one do we check first? The radio? Doris and Claude's house? The cottages?"

"All of them," Miles rumbled.

"You want us to split into three groups?" Patrick asked.

"Four if you count Erik and Jackie," Miles answered, "but yeah."

Theo shook his head. "Just like in a horror movie."

Everyone turned to the horror author then fell into silence.

"A valid point," Patrick finally said.

"Do we go for efficiency," Gillian asked, "or safety in numbers?"

"Look, vote what you like," Miles said, "but I'm checking those cottages. One of them has to have something."

He wouldn't make eye contact with Gillian. Embarrassed at his lack of faith in her idea.

"I'll come with you," Rob said.

And the decision was made.

"I'll be going to the maintenance man's house," Sabrina said, backing her own idea, arms crossed and daring anyone to tell her no.

Gillian nodded, accepting the decisions. "Doris will be there at least."

Sabrina gave a curt nod. "Anyone coming along?"

Abby bit at her lip, eyes darting to the other options. "I'll come."

Sabrina closed her eyes a moment, obviously not liking to be saddled with the person panicking most. "*Anyone else?*"

"Yeah." Theo raised a hand. "Me too."

"I'll go with Gillian," Patrick said, turning to Nick. "That just leaves you and Lisa."

"I'm going back to the cabin," Lisa said. "To see if Ben came back."

Nick looked at her and shrugged. "I was going to join Miles and Rob, but it's probably not a good idea to be alone. I'll go with Lisa."

Lisa gave him a smile and placed one hand on his arm. "Thank you, Nick. I'll be fine. I'll check the cabin then head to the office to join Pat and Gillian."

"I don't know, Lisa. I'd feel better—."

"Nick," Lisa spoke in a lower voice. "I... also need something from my bag."

Nick cocked his head, not understanding.

"A *monthly* something." Both her eyebrows shot up, chin dropping. "You know?"

"Ohhhhhh," Nick blushed with sudden understanding. "Right. Gotcha. Okay."

Nothing shut a guy up like talking about menstruation. Nick looked to Rob and Miles and nodded a *looks like I'm going with you after all.*

"Let's meet back here," Gillian said. "Thirty minutes?"

"Not here," Miles said. "Too cramped. The office?"

"That's not cramped?" Theo asked.

"Well..." Miles shrugged.

Everyone got it though. The office was an official place, where you went when there was a problem. It was instilled in them.

"The office it is," Sabrina decided. "Let's go if we're going."

Outside the groups split and went their separate ways. The sun had lowered in the sky but hadn't disappeared yet. Everyone turned on the flashlights, a precaution against all bogeymen or creeping shadows. Gillian and Patrick stood at the entry to the staff lounge, watching their friends disperse. She let out a long frustrated sigh and started back toward the office.

"They'll be okay," Patrick said.

"You sure about that? I mean, we don't know what's going on. How can splitting up be the smart move?"

A shrug. It was hopeful thinking. A wish that the only thing that was happening was a bizarre growth of trees and one destroyed phone. "We can cover more options this way. Maybe find a solution quicker."

"It's like Theo said, this if the stupid thing they do in horror movies."

Patrick was quiet a moment. "You think we're in a horror movie?"

She glanced around for their friends who were already out of sight.

"Maybe not the movie part."

"Gillian—"

"We should have stayed together, but we're all adults. Not much we can do except focus on our task."

CHAPTER

NINE

Erik pointed the flashlight left and right as he went, making sure the path was clear. Twisting an ankle wouldn't do any good, especially if it was him twisting. Here under the cover of trees night felt much further on its way and the growing dimness pressed closer with each second. They'd rushed down the path, passed a newer pool, and plunged into a path between the trees.

Jackie shone her own light to either side as they went, and occasionally back the way they'd come. Neither admitted why she was checking behind but here in the trees there was a feeling they were not alone. It was silly of course. They'd each spent several summers here and had never had such feelings.

But today they both did.

Maybe not so silly.

Overgrown bushes lined the path on either side, allowing three feet of clearance for them to walk. Neither wasted time, moving as quickly as possible with the goal in mind. This path wound along until it reached the campsites. Four areas, one after another, used for overnight campouts and picnic Sundays when the camp split into four groups and cook hamburgers over open fires, the oldest getting the honor of walking furthest.

"Almost there," Erik said.

"Yeah?"

"Looks like a clearing ahead."

Jackie continued to check the path to either side. She'd never truly enjoyed coming down here. The overnight campouts had been the worst. Well, not the campout itself, just getting there really. It had been many years since she had stood surrounded by the woods after dark and with good reason.

Why had she volunteered to come with Erik? No, she knew why. There'd been an overwhelming sense that those trees that had taken the road would keep creeping closer. Better to do this by choice.

"Look!"

She brought her flashlight around to illuminate the clearing ahead. They stepped forward, taking in the familiar scene. A big wooden shack on the left, really just a box with cut-out windows, and a circle of stones for the campfire. Off to the right a shallow stream burbled past each of the sites, headed who knew where.

Erik shook it off. "Three more of these and then the path to the road beyond that."

"You sure?"

"Unless they closed it off, but Gillian would have said

something," Erik thought a moment then sighed. "I used to have a townie guy from Millersville who would drop stuff off."

"Stuff?"

"You know. Weed. Booze," he shrugged.

Jackie looked at him stunned.

"Oh, come on. I sold this stuff to a bunch of people. Made a nice profit too. Anyway, the path is off to the left after the last site."

The two stood a moment longer, flashlights skimming the area, unsure what they hoped to see. Other than the shack and the fire pit there wasn't much except for a long-ago downed tree all the kids sat on while eating their burgers. In the summer, tents would be erected for sleepovers, but those had been taken down and stored for the season.

"Let's go," she said.

Without so much as a nod Erik headed for the path that continued on the far side, passing back into the bush. They travelled another two minutes, just long enough to get out of sight of the previous campground then out into the next. They shone the flashlights around, exposing a similar shack and fire pit. Another downed tree.

"Looks the same," Jackie said.

"It does, yeah."

"I remember each site being a bit different."

Erik fell silent, swinging the flashlight in a slow arc across the open area. Jackie was right. In fact, he thought the shack at the second site should have been to their right.

"It's been a couple of decades since we've been here," he said. "They must have moved stuff around."

"I guess."

With a shrug and an unspoken agreement, they continued on. Into the path opposite and through to the third campsite.

"Same again," Jackie muttered.

Erik spun a full circle, pointing the flashlight everywhere. It *was* the same. Exactly. Down to the felled tree to one side of the fire pit. It was something Erik didn't want to acknowledge because it was crazy but Jackie was right. These weren't just similar, but identical.

Jackie walked over to the long tree lying against the ground, an old maple, and shone her light along it.

"What is it?" he asked.

She reached out and grabbed a piece of bark which had lifted. It came away in a long strip, the sound of tearing wood filling the clearing to expose bare wood underneath.

"Why—?" Erik began.

"Probably just a stupid thought."

She didn't drop the length of bark but turned and continued toward the path which would lead to the next and final site. Erik came along behind her and they rushed into the next clearing which looked the same.

Again.

"Could they have arranged it so they all looked the same?"

"Except for this tree I might agree." Jackie crossed the clearing.

Erik joined her, his beam lighting the exposed piece of tree flesh where a strip of bark had been removed recently. "Impossible."

"Impossible or not..." She slid the piece if bark back into place, fitting it perfectly. "This is supposed to be the last site, right?"

"Yeah, there were four. I remember that much."

"Then why is there another path?" She pointed her flashlight across the clearing to another space between the bushes, another path.

"No." Erik swung his flashlight left, lighting the trees on that side of the clearing. "There should be a thin trail leading toward the road from here instead."

"Should be."

He pointed to the following path and started forward.

"Where are you going?"

"We need to see what comes next."

"Do we?"

"I do."

Jackie sighed. "Lead the way."

Erik rushed down the next path and tumbled out into another exact copy of the campsite. Across was another clearing in the bushes leading to the next campsite. He rushed for that one and down the path, out into the same site again.

"Erik, what—?"

"Stay there."

"What?"

He crossed to the path, rushed between the open bushes.

"Don't leave me here," Jackie protested.

Erik ignored her and continued along the path, spilling into an opening, staring at the back of Jackie who stared at the cleared spot he'd just travelled down.

"Fuck me!" he spat.

Jackie jumped and spun around. "Holy shit, Erik!"

She pointed at the path with her flashlight then back again to him, scanned the open area and shook her head.

"What is going on?"

"Something doesn't want us to leave."

"What do we do?"

"I... think we'd better get back to the others."

Interlude 2 – 20 Years Ago – The Axe-Man

"LUTHOR LIVED in these woods long before Camp White Bear was ever built. He enjoyed the peaceful existence and the quiet of nature. Then we came and brought a big clanging bell with us."

The kids nodded. The bell was a daily reality, waking them every morning and calling them to meals three times a day. It was just something they took for granted, bizarre on arrival but quickly becoming normalized.

The counsellors in the room, Nick and Lisa, nodded their agreement.

"What did Luthor do in the woods?" Mary-Louise asked.

Mary-Louise was the female equivalent of Jaspal in Rob's cabin. Inquisitive, sharp, and loving a good scary story. Nothing stereotypical about this girl.

"Well, Luthor did a bunch of farming. Mostly to feed himself through the winter. He made furniture from trees he cut down and sold them at the farmer's market in Millersville."

"Let me guess, he used an axe."

Theo chuckled. "Don't get ahead of me Mary-Louise."

"Sorry." She smiled but the expression said she wasn't all that sorry.

"Yes, Luthor had a shining double-bladed steel axe that he kept sharp enough to split a hair in two."

Mary-Louise nodded her approval. Theo saw a bit of himself in this girl. Staff wasn't supposed to have favorites, but everyone did and Mary-Louise would be one of his.

"The noise that came from building the camp was one thing. Luthor didn't mind the sound of construction. It was like tree cutting and furniture building but on a greater scale, and temporary. No, what he hated was what came afterwards."

"The bell?" Sarah asked.

"Exactly. It rang in the morning. Thirty times to wake everyone up. Every day. It rang again at breakfast. At lunch. At dinner. Other random times. Each ding of that bell vibrated in Luthor's soul until he could feel it eroding his mind."

"Crazy!" Mary-Louise said.

"Oh, yes. But somehow Luthor made it through that first summer, running his fingers across his bald head whenever that bell rang, as if he could keep the sound from getting in. The children went home, silence returned and he felt his sanity slide back into place."

"Until...?" Sarah asked.

"Until... in the fall someone returned to camp and started ringing the bell. It reached thirty and Luthor braced himself for the end, but it kept going. Thirty-five. Forty. Forty-five. Fifty.

This was too much for Luthor.

Luthor grabbed his gleaming axe and went for a walk."

Mary-Louise nudged Sarah and both girls giggled. Theo spoke to the whole room but his attention kept returning to these two girls. The perfect audience. Two favorites?

"When Luthor got to camp the bell was *still* being rung. He'd lost count how many clanging banging intrusions had echoed through the air. His sanity had ebbed to nothing by the time he stepped onto camp holding his axe like he was ready to chop down a tree.

Instead of a tree he found a man in coveralls ringing the bell again and again. The camp's maintenance man. In his spare hand he held a bottle of some brown coloured liquid. A second one sat next to the bell's base, empty.

Ding!

Ding!

Ding!

Ding!"

With each ding Theo slapped the mattress he sat on, creating a muffled thump that filled the cabin.

"Ding!

Luthor had lost any thought in his head other than stopping that incessant noise. He came up beside the maintenance man and swung that axe without a second thought. It connected with the bell-ringer's neck to separate it from his shoulders.

Ding!

It was the final ring of the bell.

Luthor looked at the man lying in two parts at his feet. He wiped the blood from his axe against the dead man's denim coveralls before turning and walking away, back toward his cabin."

"He just left the body?" another girl, Laurie, asked.

"That's right. Left it there in the dust for someone else to discover. On the way back home, he considered what he'd done. He felt calm. The maintenance man's death was in return for his peace being broken all summer long. He found that payment acceptable. Once every summer."

"Isn't this camp like a hundred years old?" Mary-Louise asked. "He would be crazy old now."

"Good point," Theo said. "Good point."

Nuts! He hadn't thought that far. Time to wing it.

"Each death released some ancient mountain magic on old Luthor. It took years off of him. That's why he can never stop. To stop would be his death."

"So, he's still out there?" Laurie asked, eyes going to the door.

"Oh, yes. And he hasn't taken his payment yet this summer."

A scratching noise came from the other side of the cabin. Everyone looked at Nick who held up both hands in a *not me* gesture. It came again. They looked to Lisa who shook her head.

"Not me." Did she sound a bit worried herself?

Everyone looked toward the window while Nick stared at Theo, one eyebrow raised. Theo shrugged.

A shadow moved past the window and several of the kids let out a quick scream. Mary-Louise and Sarah were on their feet and headed for the door.

"Let's catch him!"

"Wait!" Theo tried.

Before anyone could do more to stop them the two girls had the door open and were outside.

"Shit," Theo muttered.

"There!" Mary-Louise yelled. "Get him!"

"We got you Luthor!" Sarah said.

How the hell could two ten-year-old girls be so utterly fearless?

Inspired by those girl's bravery the other kids poured out of the cabin in pursuit. There were shouts and a scream. Theo knew immediately he couldn't avoid getting into shit for this one. He followed Nick and Lisa to the door and found two cabins of kids swarming over a dark shape.

"What the hell?" it bellowed.

"We got the axe-man," Laurie yelled, brave in a group.

"Um, that's just Miles," Theo said.

"The sports guy?"

"Afraid so."

Theo hoped none of them thought to question why Miles was dressed all in black. He'd recruited the guy to make some noises, to accentuate his story.

"Well, I think that's it for story-time," Lisa said. "Bed-time girls."

"Yeah, come on guys," Nick said, rounding up his boys.

Theo shook his head, wondering where it had all gone wrong.

"Thank Theo for the story," Lisa said.

Mary-Louise and Sarah both rushed up and gave him a hug.

"Thanks, Theo," Mary-Louise said. Then in a low voice only he and Sarah could have possible heard. "Next time have Miles bring an axe."

Theo's mouth dropped open. It was a damn good thing there was no axe involved tonight or his days at Camp White Bear may have been over.

TEN

Sabrina marched up to the maintenance man's house, Abby and Theo travelling in her wake. None of them had said a word since leaving the others and both Theo and Abby questioned why they'd gone along with Sabrina in the first place. Well... maybe not Theo. He knew he wanted to be close to Abby, to see how happy her marriage actually was. Not that he was thinking about rekindling the old flame but... well, he wasn't *not* thinking about it either.

The two-storey house stood just off the main camp property, closer to the dining hall than anything else. It was one of the rare homes on the mountain that was intended for year-round use and as such the maintenance people over the years had built it up, including an attached garage.

Sabrina rang the doorbell, following up with a knock on the door with the heel of her hand, the sound loud in the almost-evening air. Twenty seconds passed.

Abby said: "Maybe they aren't home?"

Sabrina shook her head. "Doris wasn't in the dining hall. Where else would she go?"

Theo looked through the small glass window of the garage. "There's a car in there. One of them must be home. Nearby at least."

Sabrina repeated her action, this time with a closed fist, like a police officer might do at the house of a suspect. When still no answer came after a half minute she tried the door latch. It opened without trouble, swinging into the silent room beyond.

"Sabrina," Abby said. "Maybe we should—"

"Should what? Wait for something bad to happen then react?"

Abby stepped back, eyes wide. For a moment Sabrina looked embarrassed but then shook it off and stepped through the doorway.

"Brr," Abby said.

The inside temperature was colder than the outside air.

Sabrina flicked the switch next to the door which did nothing.

"Power out?" Theo said.

Sabrina huffed out a breath. "Figures."

All three flicked on their flashlights and eased into the house a little further, revealing details as they went. The entry was narrow, a mirror on the left with a table and wicker basket. Hardwood flooring started at the front door and seemed to lead through the house, past a set of stairs a few feet ahead.

"Two sets of keys in this basket," Theo said.

"So, they *are* nearby," Sabrina observed. "What did Gillian say his name was?"

"Claude."

"Claude?" Sabrina called to the darkened house. "Doris?"

The only response was her own echoed voice.

"I don't like this," Abby said.

Theo shook his head in agreement.

"Like it or not, this is our only option," Sabrina said.

"We could go back to the others."

"And tell them what? The house was dark so we gave up?"

Abby looked to the doorway behind them and shrugged.

"We're already here," Theo said. "Let's take a look and see if they have a working phone."

The hallway extended past the stairs and opened into a living room. The last hazy bits of sundown came through a window to fill the room with vague shadows. Flashlight beams swept across the room to show more details. A monster-sized television was mounted on the far wall, several sizes too large for the room. Matching leather couch, love seat, and recliner occupied the room, all pointing at the huge TV. The couch pressed against the right wall with matching loveseat facing it from the other side. The recliner had its back to them on the nearer edge of the couch.

"Shit!" Sabrina spat.

Abby focussed her light where Sabrina had, revealing a wall with some sort of rack. "What?"

"Those clips are to hold rifles," Theo explained.

"Oh, well, where are they?"

Sabrina rolled her eyes and went left, passing behind the couch, ignoring Abby.

"That's the problem, Abby," Theo said. "There's no rifle there."

"Oh, I see."

Abby wasn't worried about that yet. She didn't see anything a gun would have protected them from. What were they going to do, shoot the trees? She passed to the right of the recliner, playing her light across the living room—

And screamed.

Theo and Sabrina spun to find Abby in the center of the room, flashlight pointed at the recliner in her shaking hand. The other two joined their beams with Abby's to light up the recliner, coming around for a better angle.

"Jesus!" Theo said.

The recliner's back was splattered with blood, the seat soaked. Far too much blood for someone to have simply cut themselves and gone off for a band-aid. A deep gash was torn into the leather back exposing the springs and stuffing beneath. No, there was enough blood here to fill a bucket.

Theo spun back the way they'd come, sure that someone would be there but finding only empty hallway. "We should close that door."

"Maybe," Sabrina half agreed. "Or that may just slow down our exit."

Theo glanced from the door to her and back again, then went and closed it. His hand hovered over the lock a moment, considering Sabrina's words. In the end he walked away.

"What happened here?" Abby wailed.

Sabrina shrugged. "Nothing good."

"Let's leave!"

"Go if you want to," Sabrina said without a glance. "I'm looking for that phone."

"But—"

Sabrina spun on her. "Oh, just go. It's not like you're contributing."

Abby took another step back under the force of Sabrina's vehemence.

Sabrina took a step forward. "Why did you come with me anyway?"

"I—"

"No, *I'll* tell *you* why. Just like twenty years ago you need to link up with people more capable than you."

"That's not true."

Sabrina scoffed and turned away.

"Theo?" Abby asked, her voice small and frail.

He jumped at the sound of his name and turned away from the entry behind them. "Um... Yeah, a phone."

He reached out one hand to Abby who took it. She took a deep breath and gave him a quick nod. Together they scanned the room but found no solution. No phone on the wall. No rifle in a corner waiting to be returned to the wall.

"Okay," Sabrina said. "Let's keep looking."

Abby made a small whimpering noise and pressed closer to Theo. Sabrina led the way through a doorway into the next room, a kitchen. Open concept had this and the following dining room as one large area. The kitchen had cabinets all around the walls and a wide, irregular shaped island in the center. Again, no phone, but a butcher's block of knives sat next to a toaster oven on the counter. Sabrina walked around to grab one and stopped in her tracks.

"What is it?" Theo asked.

She just shook her head.

Theo came around with Abby so close she was practically his shadow. He stopped next to Sabrina, light pointed at the floor. In the center, not far from the oven, was the severed lower half of a woman's arm. The hand wore a wedding ring with a green stone at its center.

ELEVEN

Lisa moved toward the cabin they were supposed to all share that night. During the summer it could house ten kids comfortably plus a counsellor and junior-counsellor. It would be cramped with the twelve of them in there, and no one had wanted the top bunk except for Erik and Nick, reliving their childhoods.

Shadows had taken over by the time Lisa got there, making every corner of the cabin sinister, potentially hiding something. She swung the flashlight in an arc, nose wrinkling at the smell of the place. Unwashed children, sunscreen, bug spray and just the faintest trace of urine. So familiar and so unbelievable that she spent entire summers here without noticing.

Her nose was more refined these days it seemed.

Whatever. None of that was the reason she'd returned to the cabin.

She hated to deceive them, especially Nick who was sweet and concerned about her safety. She needed to be alone though.

Lisa rushed to her lower bunk and reached under, pulling the leather overnight bag out. Sitting on the mattress she pulled it to her lap and unzipped the bag. A slight tremor to her hands.

"Come on, come on."

It was fine. She was fine.

Her blood-sugar levels were out of whack. Stress always did that to her. She just needed her injection, was more than an hour overdue in fact. She should have done this before dinner but everyone was here and she didn't want to have to admit just how badly diabetes had its hooks into her.

She feared they would all think it was deserved. The fat girl is a diabetic, what a shock!

Or was that her own internal voice talking?

Her insulin was at the bottom of the bag and Lisa found it with little effort. Getting the container open was another matter. A struggle with the packaging because shaky hands didn't help.

Practice allowed her to ready the needle and inject herself. It hurt more than usual but that was fine. In a few moments her symptoms would subside and she would be able to function again.

Maybe she could confide in one of them about all of this. Nick, maybe?

Lisa glanced toward the window. The angle looked toward the trees and office. She should have been able to see the road from here, or at least the clearing headed toward it, but now all she saw were overgrown trees.

What the hell could cause trees to grow up like that? By itself it was a strange mystery, but add the smashed phone and it went from mystery to something darker.

Stability had started to return to her body, the shakiness pushed aside again. For now.

She could join Pat and Gillian now.

CLUNK!

Lisa jumped.

The noise had come from outside, just around back. She debated calling out then decided she wasn't sure she wanted to do that. Was it someone trying to scare her? If so she wasn't going to give the satisfaction. Was it whoever had smashed the phone...?

She was painfully aware she was alone. Just like every big breasted bimbo in a horror movie who goes off by themselves. She should have let Nick come with her after all.

CLUNK!

Something bumped up against the outside wall of the cabin.

She considered dropping to the floor and rolling under the bunk.

CREAK!

The sound of metal grinding against metal as the door knob was twisted in the door. Slowly. Agonizingly. Did she have time to drop and roll?

No.

The door flew open, slamming against the inside wall with a noise that reverberated in the growing evening.

Standing framed in the doorway was the shadow of a thin figure, outlined by light from behind.

"Found you," it said.

CHAPTER

TWELVE

A dirt path led past the dining hall, winding its way toward a road which continued deeper up the mountain. A road which should have gone all the way down the mountain in the other direction, but now ended in a wall of trees.

Cottages had started to be built here around the same time as Camp White Bear itself. Between where they stood now and the far end of that road were hundreds of cozy two and three bedroom cottages. The first of them a ten minute walk from camp property.

Nick always wondered what those occupants closest to camp thought about the noise in the summer. They used a great bell for waking the kids in the morning and he couldn't imagine anyone being okay with that, like that axe-guy from Theo's story.

"Which one do we try?" Rob asked.

Miles shrugged. "First one we come to I guess."

Rob nodded. "Makes sense."

"Maybe we'll find Ben too," Nick added.

Neither Miles or Rob had a response to that, all of them wondering if they would ever actually see Ben again. That led to thoughts of whether anyone would actually ever see *them* again. Would they just be a disappearance mystery like that one in Roanoake?

The three headed along the path, past the dining hall, past a shed for maintenance equipment and a small farm tended by the summer staff and children, then up a slight rise and between two gates.

"There," Nick said, pointing at the first building which came into view.

Miles slowed, staring at this first cottage. He looked back the way they'd come and forward again, coming to a stop.

"Something wrong?" Rob asked.

"I don't remember cottages starting so close to camp."

The other two came to a stop, looking back.

"It does seem close." Nick admitted. "Maybe they're new?"

Miles shook his head. "I thought this was still camp property though."

"When we get back to Gillian's office we can check the map on the wall," Rob said.

Miles looked at him. "What map?"

"You didn't see it? It was some old property map of camp. Patrick almost knocked it off the wall."

A shake of his head and Miles returned his attention toward the cottage. With a shrug he started forward again.

Nick and Rob fell into step beside him. As the trio approached the cottage still more came into view further along the road. All of them were equally dark and lifeless. The summer residents had given up for the year and locked up against the coming winter.

"I always wondered why people locked up their cabins so early," Rob said. "There's still lots of nice days left."

"Trees changing colour and all that," Nick agreed. "You're right."

It was always like there was some unspoken agreement that once the middle of September came that everything shut down and the residential cottages would be left until late spring. A mass exodus of all the summer people.

"So do we just break in?" Rob asked.

Miles didn't even slow, going to the door and trying the handle. Locked of course. The door itself was a solid thing with a set of nine glass panes looking back at them. Beyond they could see a sun room attached to the front of this cottage.

"Well, either we break in or keep trying doors until we find a cottage that's unlocked."

Miles didn't wait for response from his two companions, as if the answer to these options was obvious. Sleeve down to cover his right hand he punched through the lower left pane then knocked the remaining shards away before letting his hand free again. He reached through and searched for the lock. With a click it was free and swung into the dimness of the inside.

Wicker chairs and couches were arranged in the sun room ready for the occupants to take coffee in the morning.

The seat cushions were gone though, put away for the winter.

"Why are these not broken into more?" Nick wondered.

Miles shrugged. "Who would do it? Other cottage owners?"

"People who are trapped by supernatural tree growth?" Rob said.

A joke no one found funny.

"Supernatural?" Miles asked.

"Well, what else?" Rob said. "Trees don't just sprout up like that, do they?"

"No," Miles agreed. "That is impossible."

"Well then—"

"You're saying magic?" Nick asked.

"I don't know what it is. Magic. Hand of God. Nature attacks. Who knows."

"Does it matter why?" Miles asked.

"Maybe," Rob answered. "If we knew why maybe we would know what to do about it."

Another shrug and Miles stepped further into the cottage, light flashing around to light up the living room inside. An attached kitchen sat just off of it in an open concept more for function than style. Toward the back four rooms lined a hallway, all doors closed.

Rob crossed the room and grabbed the phone receiver, holding it to his ear while the other two looked at him expectantly. He shook his head.

"Dead."

"Looks like a consistent theme where the phones are concerned," Miles said.

"You think all the cottages will be the same?" Rob asked.

"I do."

"No help from outside then."

Miles shook his head.

"What do we do then?"

"Look for weapons?"

The three glanced around at the small cottage. Magazines littered the small coffee table, ready for next summer's return of the owners. Nothing on the kitchen counters except for airtight sugar, flour, and coffee containers. Not even a decoration on the wall of a sword or anything.

"Do we check all the drawers?" Nick asked. "Or move on to the next one?"

"I vote next cottage," Rob said. "There's nothing here."

"Maybe in one of the bedrooms?" Nick suggested.

"Nah," Miles agreed with Rob. "These aren't the kind of people who have a hidden gun. Even if they did, they would have taken it with them."

"Baseball bat?" Nick suggested.

"Hmm," Miles shrugged. "Try the closet."

Nick rushed over to the door and opened it. Empty.

Did they try the rooms or just get going?

"Right," Nick agreed. "Next cottage then."

The three returned to the road and travelled the minute or so to the next residence in line. Another broken window. No sun room on this one and a different layout inside, but much the same contents. Another dead phone. Another useless cottage.

As was the next.

"Is there any point to this?" Rob asked.

Miles considered the question and shrugged. "One more?"

"Sure," Rob agreed, though with less enthusiasm and hope than he had for the first place they'd come to.

They walked another minute to the next house.

"Something is different," Miles said.

The flashlights landed on the cottage's entry, showing a front door which had been splintered inward. Shards of wood and glass littered the floor beyond.

"This is familiar," Rob said.

Nick looked away from the entry. "Familiar how?"

"I've been here."

"Ben's cottage?"

"I think so… But this should be like fifteen minutes away."

"What happened here?" Nick asked.

Neither one had an answer for that.

"Come on," Miles said.

Rob and Nick came up behind him. The three creeping toward the shattered door. Beyond was a sun room entry similar to the first place only this one had been torn apart.

"Looks like the Tasmanian Devil came through here," Rob said.

Miles continued on, passing into the main part of the cottage. The three once again swung their lights across the open area. Living room. Kitchen. Hallway leading to—

"Shit," Nick said, flashlight shaking in his hands making the beam dance.

Miles and Rob brought their lights around to join his.

"Jesus," Rob said. "What the fuck?"

Miles shook his head. "Aw, man, Ben."

At the narrow hallway leading to bedrooms and bathroom was their missing friend. He'd been nailed to the wall on either side by his hands and feet, splayed out in an X shape.

CHAPTER

THIRTEEN

Lisa was on her feet, flashlight shaking in her hands. She backed away from the owner of that voice, though there wasn't much space for her to back up into. The outline in the doorway stood unmoving while in the last few moments the sun decided to complete its descent. The backlight disappeared and Lisa whipped the flashlight around to illuminate the intruder.

"Ben?"

He shuffled forward, his gaze never quite meeting her eyes, his back hunched forward. All the mannerisms she expected from him... or what she would have expected all those years ago. Had he not changed at all?

"You scared me."

"Sorry, Lisa."

He came closer, stopping a couple of feet from her.

"Where have you been? We looked all over for you."

"You did?"

"Well, Erik did. He wanted to apologize."

"He didn't look hard. I came here."

Lisa shook her head, she should have known better from Erik.

"The road is gone," Ben said, turning back toward the door a moment and cocking a finger toward the missing road.

"The cars too," Lisa added.

"Right. Right. What's going on?"

"No one knows."

"No one knows," Ben repeated, head cocked to one side. "Where are the others?"

Lisa got her breathing back under control, her heartbeat slowed. "Gillian and Patrick went looking for a radio. Erik and Jackie are trying to get to the road another way to get cell service."

"Smart idea, but that won't work."

"How do you know?"

A shrug. "Where did the rest go?"

"Umm... the maintenance man's house or the residential cottages."

"The cottages?"

"Yeah, they're hoping for a phone or some weapons."

"Weapons?"

"Is your parent's cottage close?"

"Parent's cottage?"

"Yeah, you said you were checking on it while you were up here."

"I did, didn't I?"

Lisa stared at her old friend, getting a creepy feeling. He kept parroting her words without adding anything of his own. Was it possible he was on something? Was that where he'd gone after fleeing the dining hall?

"The cottage is close," Ben said. "Easy to get to."

"Is there a phone?"

"A phone? It won't be working."

"What?"

"The phones are dead."

"How do you know?"

"There's no one to call."

A chill ran through her body. "Yeah but—"

"Who's the leader?"

"The leader? You mean Gillian?"

"Gillian... Yes..."

"Ben, are you okay? You're acting weird."

"You were always kind to Ben."

"I..." Had he just referred to himself in the third person?

"Good memories. Cherished. Strong."

Lisa took a step back, light trained on Ben once again. The window was at her back and the door, the only real exit, was on this increasingly creepy man.

"Ben, you're freaking me out here."

"Memories are like a nectar."

The light showed heavy menacing shadows around Ben's features, making him look like a different person entirely. His face shifted, eyes a flat grey color, before it all resolved into Ben once again.

"Ben always cared for you."
Ben took a step forward.
Lisa took a step back, raising the flashlight a bit.
Her eyes darted left and right, looking for a way around.

FOURTEEN

The storage area was located underneath the office and only accessible from the outside, around back. Patrick and Gillian stared at the locked door. Solid and serious.

"I hope you have the key," Patrick said.

Gillian produced a keyring of perhaps a dozen keys from inside her jacket pocket. With practiced ease she separated one from the others and unlocked the door. Inside they walked hunched over, avoiding banging their heads against the low ceiling. The flick of a switch lit one lone bulb exposing the room's contents as mostly a mass of banker's boxes stacked from floor to ceiling.

"Paperwork," Gillian said with a shrug, placing one hand on the nearest box. "Going back to those first campers a hundred years ago. These days it's all saved on computer, a condition of the government grants we receive." Gillian sounded as if she was giving a tour. "Interesting stuff. A few recognizable names, both campers and staff, who went on to be somewhat famous."

"Very cool," Patrick looked around. "Where's the radio?"

Gillian chuckled "You seem nervous."

He turned toward his old friend, wondering if she was trying to be ironic or make a joke. She looked back at him as if his concerns were indeed strange.

"Well, Gillian, the road has disappeared along with our cars. One phone has been destroyed and the other isn't working. It seems like something sinister might be going on. How are you *not* nervous?"

She looked aside, as if considering his perspective. "I don't know... I guess Camp White Bear is the one place where I've always felt safe."

Patrick nodded. Until today he would have agreed. "Let's just find the radio."

"It's over here." Gillian went to a table holding an odd sheet-covered shape, the one thing definitely not another box of paper. She pulled the covering aside and exposed a radio that was ancient when they worked here.

"Does it work?"

"Last time I tried it."

"How long ago was that?"

Gillian considered. "I really don't remember. Sometime before I became camp director."

"At least five years then?"

She nodded. "Six in December."

"Happy anniversary."

"Thank you," She smiled. "If you carry it to the office, we can plug it in."

Patrick slipped his flashlight into one pocket and grabbed the radio by handles on either side. The weight of it took him by surprise.

"Heavier than it looks," Gillian said.

Bracing his knees and back he tried again, and was able to lift it from the solid table with a groan of effort. No space to walk normally in the cramped room he duck walked with the radio. Gillian rushed over and held the door.

"Thing weighs a ton," he grunted, side-shuffling through the doorway.

"Hey!" she said and rushed away, coming back with a wheelbarrow that had leaned up against the wall. "Will this help?"

"God, yes!"

With another groan, this time of relief, Patrick plunked the radio down inside it then rested against the door to catch his breath.

"That will... definitely... make it easier."

Gillian nodded. "Want me to take a turn?"

"Gillian, you're a strong woman. Mentally. Emotionally. But you've got skinny toothpick arms."

"Toothpick?" She laughed out loud then glanced at each arm and shrugged. "I'll get the doors then?"

The terrain was uneven, and uphill. The radio would certainly bounce around a bit but it seemed sturdy enough to survive that.

"You really think I'm strong?"

"Hell, yes. You took this camp, which was struggling financially, and built it up over the past five years. You're amazing."

"Aw, thank you. Donations like yours make the difference each year."

Arms recovered Patrick bent to grab the handles of the wheelbarrow. It rolled forward grudgingly under the weight of the radio. Still, it was better than breaking his back. Once the momentum was built it shouldn't be as much struggle, unless the wheel hit soft earth and the greater weight pressed it down into mud. Then they'd be screwed.

One step. Two steps.

A giggle came from the darkness, to their right and behind. Both spun, pointing their flashlights in the direction.

"I don't see anything," Gillian whispered.

Another giggle.

Not the giggle of a child. No, this was the giggle of an adult who might have more than one thing wrong inside of their head.

It reminded Patrick of something but he couldn't decide what.

The giggles continued but didn't come closer, the owner of those giggles wasn't exposing themselves.

"Who is there?" Gillian demanded.

"Who's the slooooooowpoke?" a voice called, high and definitely mad.

"No," Patrick said.

"That's... Those words..."

"Yeah, I know the giggle now."

"The old cook?"

Patrick called. "Theo? Is that you?"

Another giggle. No answer.

Gillian shook her head. "That's not Theo."

"No."

"We should go."

Patrick pushed the wheelbarrow a little quicker, up a slight incline, heading for the front of the office. "Quick Gillian."

"What the hell's going on here Pat?"

"I don't know. Just keep moving."

No answer. Just the huff of exertion as Gillian kept up.

"It was like Doris said at lunch. The mad cook would grab a kid and make them into hamburger."

A grunt of acknowledgement.

"The slowest kid," he said, dropping the wheelbarrow at the top of the incline. "The one at the back of the line. Gillian!"

Patrick spun to find himself alone.

Gillian was gone.

FIFTEEN

Rob stepped closer to Ben while behind him Nick made a gurgling sound, as if getting closer was an impossible concept. Miles was just quiet, completely out of character for him.

"We need to get him down," Rob said.

"We need to get the fuck out of here," Miles answered.

"This is our friend!" Rob's tone was shocked, offended.

"Someone powerful and completely insane did this. We need to get back and warn the others."

"But—"

"Look, Ben is beyond caring now. We can come back in the morning when this is all done and take care of him then."

"In the morning," Nick chimed in. "What makes you think this will all be over?"

Miles shrugged. "It will all be over or..."

"Or," Rob finished, "we'll all be like Ben."

Miles didn't answer. It seemed bad luck to say such a thing out loud.

"We came looking for a phone," Nick said, "and weapons. "Do we continue?"

Miles looked around the small space of the family cottage and shook his head.

"Don't bother," Rob said. "Ben's dad was a total pacifist. I remember the drive up here and listening to him going on about gun violence."

"A phone then," Nick suggested.

Miles sighed. "Sixty seconds and then I am out of here."

Nick stepped into the open kitchen, sweeping the flashlight around while Miles headed for the living room. It wasn't as if the phone would be hidden in a drawer or anything. It should be obvious whether it was there or not. Both quietly hoped that Ben's dad had changed his mind at some point and bought a shotgun.

Rob stepped closer to their friend and looked up at him.

"Sorry, man." He said in a whisper "I wish we could take care of you now."

Ben's eyes opened.

Rob took a quick step back and tripped over his own feet, his ass smacking hard against the wood floor. One flailing arm knocked over a small table holding magazines.

"What the hell?" Nick said.

"He's alive," Rob said. "We have to get him down."

Nick and Miles rushed over as Ben's head swiveled, focussing on one then the next. His eyes were open and bugging out, lips spreading into what seemed like a smile. Blood filled the spaces between each tooth.

"Hellllooooooooo."

"He's... he's..." Rob couldn't get words out.

Nick shook his head in disbelief, his light showing their friend so savagely nailed to the wall.

"Hold on Ben," Miles managed. "We'll get you down."

"Noooooo," Ben moaned out. "Come back in the morning if you're still alive."

Then he laughed.

Teeth gritted Ben pulled his left hand forward. One moment he was hanging by both, then he slid the nail through skin and bone with a squelching noise that filled the cottage. For a moment he hung there, free arm dangling.

"This little mouse can take care of himself." Ben pulled his other hand.

"No, Ben," Rob managed, jumping up. "Your feet—"

Too late.

Ben jerked the right hand free and fell forward, his two feet still attached to the wall. Ripping flesh and cracking bone assaulted their ears as gravity and the weight of Ben's body pulled him toward the floor. The nail in his right foot came out of the wall but the left held. Ben pivoted on that nail and landed head first on the floor.

He twisted to look up at his friends, lunatic glee in his eyes, A laugh in his throat.

"Ben—" Rob began.

"That ain't Ben," Miles said.

"What are you talking about?" Rob was already leaning over the prone figure, reaching out to grab him under the arms. He wasn't sure what to do except take some of the weight off of that foot. "Come on! Help me."

Nick stepped forward but Miles grabbed him by one arm and held him back.

"Find a hammer," Rob pleaded.

"Hammer, hammer, hammer," Ben repeated.

"Ben it's—"

Ben's fingers extended to claws, the right one shooting out and plunging into Rob's stomach, arching upwards. With a quick twist the hand went deeper, digging upward until he was into Rob up to the shoulder. Another jerk of the arm and Ben pulled out Rob's heart.

It gave one last beat in Ben's fist.

Then Ben locked eyes with the other two and took a bite of the organ.

"Jesus!" Nick backed away.

The shadows around Ben's face twisted, deepening as his appearance shifted. First he looked like Nick, then for a moment Miles, before settling back into Ben's face once again.

"Better run," it told them.

Interlude 3 – 20 Years Ago – Doppelgangers

"HOW WELL DO we all know each other?" Theo asked.

The kids and counsellors looked around at each other. A couple of shrugs.

"Well enough to know if someone had been replaced with a copy?"

More glances around, some appraising glances at certain people. The unspoken question being: *How would you know if someone had been replaced?*

"That's what happened to a counsellor named Patrick. He was walking alone at night after going for a run along the lake road."

Patrick sat to one side, listening to Theo's story, and ignoring his kids who turned to glance at him. He knew he couldn't win. If he denied it was him in the story Theo would find a way to imply it was indeed him. If he admitted it might be him then he was opening a door to who knows what.

They all knew he went for a run every day.

Theo caught his eye and gave him a smile, formulating the story according to how his friend reacted. No reaction at all was still a reaction of sorts.

Challenge accepted.

"There's an old race of creature that lives in these mountains." Theo drew out the word old. Ollllllddddd. "Most of the time we don't see them at all, but once in a while they get curious."

"What kind of creature?" Patrick asked.

Theo chuckled to himself. Gotcha!

"Oh, a sneaky creature. One that can change the way it looks."

"Ah."

Theo nodded and focussed on the campers. "You see, they look for someone by themselves at night and grab them."

"And do what?" one camper asked.

This was one of Patrick's kids. Perfect! Theo had six cabins of kids he was telling this story to. Not a nighttime story but a Sunday picnic. He'd been given the task of distracting the kids while Gillian, Jackie and the new kid Erik all worked on getting the fire going and cook burgers. Patrick and Sabrina were on crowd control while he told the story. Poor Ben was on pee duty, shuttling kids to a specified tree to relieve themselves, though none were going at the moment, engrossed in the story instead.

"Well, you see, these creatures take over the lives of the people they grab. They swarm the person in greater numbers and hold them down, studying their face until they can look exactly like that person. They even absorb some of their memories, but not everything."

"And Patrick...?" another one in Patrick's cabin.

"Well, they grabbed this counsellor and studied him, completely replacing him. Then took him away to their caves."

"Why?"

"Well," Theo chuckled. "Let's say these Doppelgangers are not vegetarian."

"No!" one kid whispered.

"Yuck!" offered another.

"Afraid so."

"So what happened with this Doppelganger that replaced the counsellor?" Patrick asked.

"Well, he just fit right in. No one had any idea."

"Really?"

"Yep."

"How do we know if someone is a Doppelganger?" the kid in Patrick's cabin again, but the rest of them were nodding.

"Well, there is one way to tell."

"How? How?"

"You have to catch them unaware."

"Unaware?"

"They can't suspect it's coming or they'll be on guard."

"Okay. And do what?"

"Shine a light in their face and watch for their features to change. So, all of you be on alert."

He gave them a wink. The kids looked around at each other, at the counsellor. Mostly a bunch of eyes stared at Patrick.

"Great story, Theo," Patrick sighed. "Thanks for that."

There was a suspicion in the eyes of Patrick's kids as their gaze lingered. Theo loved them at this age. They believed so easily. Patrick was in for an interesting night.

"Oh, my pleasure," Theo laughed.

CHAPTER

SIXTEEN

The three of them stared at the severed arm, panic reaching its grasping fingers out for them.

"What do we do?" Abby demanded, hyperventilating. "What do we do?"

"We're okay, Abby," Theo said. "Calm down."

"Calm? Calm? How can I be calm?"

"Because if you aren't," Sabrina spoke in a matter-of-fact tone without looking at her, "there's a good chance you'll end up like Doris here."

Abby shut her mouth with a clack.

Sabrina turned to Theo. "This is like one of your books."

Theo nodded, glancing around.

"So, what would your characters do?"

"Do...? I don't know... I..." He stopped, took a calming breath and thought about it. "They would keep searching the house."

"And that would turn out bad."

"Probably... But if they decided to leave some other bad thing would happen."

"So, there's no good choice?"

Abby whimpered a little but tried to control it.

"If this was one of my books? No, there would be no good choice."

"This isn't a book Sabrina," Abby wailed. "This is something real and insane."

"True."

"What do we do?"

"Good question." Sabrina turned to Theo again. "You're the expert."

Theo sighed. "We continue to search. We might find a working phone or a weapon."

Abby shook her head. "I want to go back to the others."

"So go," Sabrina said and turned back toward the living room and the blood-spattered armchair.

"I'm not going alone!"

"Then stop whining."

Again Abby shut her mouth, but this time she glared at Sabrina while she did it.

Sabrina spoke to Theo, as if they were the only two there. "We should also see if Doris is maybe alive."

Theo glanced at the severed half-arm and nodded. A person *could* possibly survive an injury like that, if they could tie it off and get help. It was doubtful that anyone who would inflict such a wound would stop there though. With a glance at Abby he decided to keep that opinion to himself.

"Nothing down here," Sabrina said. "Upstairs maybe?"

Theo nodded, realizing that Sabrina had embraced the

situation. Some people came alive in stressful situations while others shut down. Theo thought he had one of each with him. Which was he though?

As one they headed for the front of the house and the stairs leading up. Each of them kept their lights away from the armchair and the massacre which had happened there.

"Maybe..." Abby said. "Maybe that armchair was Doris too?"

"What do you mean?" Theo asked.

"Well... if that blood is hers then her husband is possibly still around."

"Fair point," Sabrina agreed. "You think he did this?"

"I..." Abby tried. "I..."

"No," Theo said. "Maybe he *could* do this but that would mean he'd done the trees too. That seems a bit outside his skillset."

"Logical," Sabrina agreed. "Let's look upstairs."

Another small whimper left Abby as she glanced at the exit door, then to the stairs, weighing her options. "Your idea," Abby whispered. "*You* lead the way."

Sabrina gave a tight smile. "Fine, you can bring up the rear. You know, the one the monster always gets in the movie."

"No." It came out of Abby is a small, low voice, almost like a child.

"It's okay Abby, you go second," Theo said.

Sabrina gave him a glance and rolled her eyes. What she considered a shared acknowledgment that they were saddled with the most useless of their friends in this situation. She kept the flashlight pointed upward as they climbed the stairs, lighting the steps ahead. As they approached the top landing she slowed. There was a blind spot ahead that could hold a person, just around the corner on their left as they reached the top.

"Well, go on," Abby whispered.

Gritting her teeth against the comment she wanted to say, Sabrina crept forward, sweeping the light left as they reached the top.

Empty.

She laughed slightly with relief. Inside her own mind she now admitted that coming up here was potentially a dumb move. This gave them no avenue of escape and there was very obviously someone around doing bodily harm to people. But to turn back now would give Abby smug satisfaction and she just couldn't do it.

Plus, old Claude just might have a weapon or two upstairs.

Sabrina continued forward.

The upper floor continued in a short hallway ending with a door to either side, both closed.

"Left or right?" Sabrina asked.

"Left?" Abby answered.

Sabrina went to the door on the right and grasped the knob.

"Why even ask?" Abby said.

"I'm assuming that you would make the wrong decision so went with the opposite."

Abby's mouth pressed into a tight line as she glared at the other woman.

"Let's check both," Theo said.

"Always the peacekeeper," Sabrina said.

Theo shrugged and went to the other door. He twisted the knob and pushed it open before Sabrina could do the same on her side. Inside was a small bedroom. A double bed, a dresser and a door to a closet was all that greeted him.

"Nothing here."

Sabrina nodded and pushed the door on her side open.

Inside was a massacre.

Splayed across the queen-size bed was Doris, the stump of her left hand gleaming in the beam light. One of her legs was half-severed, drooping over the edge of the bed at an awkward angle.

Sabrina inched into the room. On the far side of the bed, pressed up against an old wooden dresser, was the cook's husband. The man's head was missing.

"Why...?" Abby said, her voice on the edge of screaming panic.

"Why what?" Sabrina snapped rounding on her. "What?"

Abby shook her head, took a breath. Her eyes didn't leave the body on the bed. "Why are they here?"

Sabrina rolled her eyes again but Theo heard something in the words. "What do you mean, Abby?

"Well, they were obviously killed downstairs," she explained. "Why drag them up here?"

Sabrina stopped at that and turned to Theo, for the first time there was a fear in her eyes.

"Fuck," she said.

Theo groaned. "They're bait."

Downstairs the front door creaked open, then slammed closed again.

SEVENTEEN

"Gillian?" Patrick called.

Silence. Nothing but the sound of wind.

"Gillian?!" he called again, louder.

A distant giggle drifted from the trees to him and Patrick felt his insides turn to water.

"This is madness."

Madder than the trees closing in and preventing their escape? Madder than the phones not working or destroyed?

A follow up giggle put Patrick into motion. He grabbed the wheelbarrow handles started forward as fast as he could move. Almost immediately the radio lurched right, attempting to throw itself into the dirt.

"Slow down, slow down."

If he capsized it he would leave the radio where it landed and book out of there, back to the office...

He couldn't though. They needed it.

Better to be careful.

The old crazy cook. Patrick tried to remember any other details from Theo's story. She would lurk in the trees, watching as the kids went past. If there was one slower than the rest, she would grab them and make them into hamburgers or something.

Was that what had happened to Gillian?

"No," he whispered. "No!"

He refused to believe that.

Coming around the office he approached the front steps, light illuminated the windows inside. Well, at least there was power. Patrick dropped both handles and the wheelbarrow slammed against the ground. The weight took it down quicker than expected. The radio lurched back a moment before settling again. He spun a tight circle, hoping to find Gillian standing there... Hoping NOT to catch a glimpse of this cook.

Nothing.

He was alone.

"Gillian!" he called again, answered by his own echo. "God damn it!"

Would that crazy old bitch come after him next? Technically he was last in line, but wasn't he also leading the way?

He grabbed the handles of the radio and jerked it from the wheelbarrow, lifting with his knees as he'd been told a million times since he was a kid. Patrick grunted with the effort. It wasn't only heavy, it was awkward, scraping against his knees as he tried to manhandle the thing up the office steps. At the top he rested the heavy thing against the railing while he got the door open, taking a look behind and around him. Still nothing, and the giggles had receded. He didn't delude himself into thinking that meant safety. This was more than just trees stopping them from leaving.

The railing creaked under the weight and he was sure he'd pushed his luck too far, but the old wood held.

With great effort and no grace whatsoever, he muscled the radio through the door and over to the inside table where its home used to be, slamming it down. Like the porch railing this piece of furniture groaned under the weight but held, as if welcoming back an old lover.

There was a plug right next to the table which accepted the cord easily. Step one completed.

"What else?"

An antenna was taped to the radio's back side.

"Where the hell does this go?"

Shoving the old radio in a half circle he found the connection at the back. It seemed obvious but Patrick needed a screwdriver to bring the two together.

"Of course I do."

He shuffled through the desks in the entry and found nothing. No screwdriver on the shelves or anything.

"Where did I see one?"

The dining hall? No.

Staff lounge? No.

With sudden inspiration he rushed through the open doorway and down the hall to Gillian's office. A screwdriver with exchangeable heads sat on her desk where he'd seen it earlier.

"Okay!"

On the way out of the office Patrick's gaze landed on the framed picture on the wall, hanging slightly askew. He hadn't looked earlier but had almost knocked it to the floor. It was yellowed with age, crumbling at the edges. A date of 1932 was printed in one corner. An old surveyor's map by the looks of it, showing camp property in its entirety.

Bigger than he expected.

No time for that now.

Back to the entry he was sure the radio would be gone, or destroyed, or the crazy cook would be waiting for him, but everything was as he'd left it. Turned out he had the right screwdriver head as well and attached the antenna. Patrick hoped that he got it right, that he wasn't missing a step. Back in the camp days the radio was always picking up stray signals from close by. Would there still be people on these radios? Could he raise the police down in Millersville?

Patrick turned the power knob with an authoritative click.

Nothing happened.

Off. On. Off. On.

"No, damn it. No!"

There was power in the building. The office lights were on. The outlets had to be working.

"What did I do wrong?"

He glanced at the door, hoping to find Gillian standing there. It had just been a mix up. She'd tripped or something.

"Yeah, sure."

Patrick grabbed the flashlight and stomped out the door, sending the strong beam left and right. He rushed back toward the storage area where the door still stood open.

"Gillian!"

Approaching the spot where he'd last seen her the light showed the details of the path.

A splash of color.

Something wet.

He leaned down to touch the spot.

Blood.

Just a few drops, but fresh.

Leading away were two small furrows in the dirt, arching toward the tall grass. Something had been dragged here, something which hadn't fought back.

"Gillian!" he called hopelessly.

The beam lit up the surrounding trees and revealed nothing.

The giggles didn't return.

He was completely alone.

Interlude 4 – 20 Years Ago – Doris, the Crazy Cook

"Who likes the food here?" Theo asked.

Some hands shot up. Some nods. No real negative reactions. Not surprising since some of these kids were used to not getting three meals a day back home.

"Hamburgers. Shepherd's pie. Pizza. Chili," he drawled. "Mmmmmm!"

A couple of laughs.

"There used to be a crazy cook here," Theo continued, looking out at his audience.

"Like Maggie?" one of Abby's kids asked.

"No, no. Not like Maggie at all."

Maggie was the new cook that summer and she really was a bit on the unstable side. Rumor was she'd done prison time and was the last person who's shit list Theo wanted to find himself on. That could lead to cold food, running out of dessert before they got to his table, dirty utensils, or who knew what else. Maggie provided his inspiration for this character but he wasn't about to admit that.

"No, this cook was named Doris."

A few nods. Did anyone actually know a Doris these days? He had an aunt with the name, who wasn't crazy at all, but the name fit well.

"For years Doris worked at the camp. Three meals a day and rarely a thank you. None of the kids knew her or stopped to say hello, but she could live with that. She was providing food for kids that didn't always get enough at home.

She was content.

Until the day one kid complained about cold porridge.

He didn't just complain, he'd called it glop. *Glop!*"

Some glances between each other. Who hadn't complained about cold porridge or burned toast?

"This complainer was a chubby boy who liked his food a bit more than his cabinmates. His name was Neville."

"I thought Neville disappeared going to the bathroom," Jaspal said.

Oops, Theo nodded his agreement. He should start making notes, if for no other reason than to keep track of what names he'd used. Some of these kids would be back again next year too. Oh well, nothing to be done about it now.

"Good memory, Jaspal. This was a different Neville."

"Glad my name isn't Neville," Jaspal muttered.

No, but Theo thought next session there might be a story featuring a kid too smart for his own good named Jaspal.

"Absolutely," Theo agreed. "Neville has always been an unlucky name here."

Hmm, a different story for later? Maybe.

"So, *this* Neville complained about the porridge on the way out of the dining hall, a little too close to the kitchen doors.

This glop is cold and awful!

Old Doris heard and made a note of the ungrateful child."

Nothing great about this story yet. Just setting it all up. Hopefully this wouldn't be one of the ones he'd regret.

"Doris might have let it all go and forgotten about Neville but something else happened that day. The delivery truck didn't arrive. Oh, they'd called to say they wouldn't make it until the next day. Problems with the truck they said. It left Doris in a bit of a pickle. She'd been counting on the hamburger meat that would be delivered to make shepherd's pie for dinner and was short by several pounds.

Neville would undoubtedly complain.

So old Doris went for a walk to think, along the road leading to the lake. She did her best thinking while walking but then she heard the sound of approaching kids. In no mood to see anyone she left the trail and waited in the bushes, just out of site.

Now, Doris had brought a burlap sack with her."

"Why would she do that?"

"Good question, Heath." Theo nodded. "You see she would sometimes collect wild berries on her walks."

"Oh."

"She also brought along her meat cleaver."

"What?" Jaspal said. "Why?"

"Well, when she got the call about the delivery, she was so upset she just left the kitchen holding her cleaver. She didn't even realize it until she stood in the bushes, listening to the sound of approaching kids."

Jaspal nodded. All the kids leaned forward. They'd accepted the hardest part. From here it was easy.

"Standing in the bushes Doris giggled to herself. She didn't even realize it. And the closer the voices came the more she giggled.

Now, you ever notice when you're out for walks that there's always one kid at the back of the line. Usually the same one."

Nods from all around. Abby placed one hand over her

mouth to hide her smile and stifle a giggle of her own. Every counsellor had that one kid that struggled to keep up with the group and drove their counsellor nuts.

"Well, guess who was at the back of the line when those kids and their counsellor came into view?"

"Neville!" Jaspal said.

"Yes, indeed.

There at the back, struggling to keep up was Neville.

The *same* Neville that called her porridge *glop!*

And that was when Doris's cheese completely slid off her cracker."

Theo tapped at his temple.

The kids and counsellors laughed at this.

"Well, old Doris waited and watched from the shadows, a plan forming in her mad mind. She waited, suppressing her giggles, until the rest of the campers had passed. Then, just as Neville came within a foot of her, she bolted forward.

Wha...? Neville managed before finding the burlap sack over his head.

Who's a slooooooowpoke? She hissed in his ear before bopping him on the head with the handle of her cleaver.

With Neville in dreamland, Doris dragged him off the road and back into the bushes.

Don't worry, Doris purred into Neville's ear. *You'll never have cold porridge again.*"

"What... What did she do?" Rebecca asked, the boldest of Abby's kids.

"Well," Theo chuckled "Let's just say that Doris was able to make shepherd's pie after all."

EIGHTEEN

Erik and Jackie rushed through the next campsite—the previous campsite really—with barely a glance. They entered the following path and on to yet another. The next should be the last, then the pool, but Jackie took a closer look and stumbled to a halt. She said nothing, allowing Erik to continue on and disappear between the bushes on the far side of the clearing. She knew what would happen. It should have been obvious from the start.

"What the hell?" a voice said from behind her.

With a nod Jackie turned to face Erik, who came up behind her now. He stopped, glancing around then sagged in defeat.

"So, we can't go back," he said.

"And we can't go forward."

"Which leaves us trapped in a loop."

"How do we get out?"

Erik considered that and shook his head. "I'm up for any suggestions."

Jackie crossed to sit on the log in front of the cold fire pit, leaning forward, head in her hands. Erik gave her space to think while he searched for alternatives of his own. No way forward, no way back. If this was the unending loop it seemed to be then they were fucked. They had no food and it would get cold tonight.

Erik fished in his jacket pocket finding wallet, keys, a lighter, and not much else. The lighter could help them keep warm, if either of them remembered how to start a fire. That was one skill he'd never mastered while working here. He'd always let others make the campfires while he cooked the burgers.

"Crap."

Jackie looked up at the sound of his voice and nodded. "I don't have any ideas, Erik."

He crossed the clearing and sat next to her, not really needing to say anything.

"Think the others are doing any better?" she asked.

"No."

Jackie jerked at the bleak judgement and turned toward him. "No?"

"No. The trees have closed in to trap us while the phones have been cut off to prevent communication. Now you and I can't get out. I'm sure whatever they're doing they are making similar progress."

She blew out a breath and nodded. "Makes sense. So do we just give up?"

Give up?

The idea of it irked Erik and he found himself back on his feet, glaring around.

"I refuse to just starve here."

"The cold will finish us first."

Erik showed her the lighter. "You remember how to start a fire?"

"I think so."

"Okay, well, let's call that plan B."

"I'd love to hear plan A."

"Me too..." He stared at the trees a moment, head cocked.

"You have an idea?"

"Not much of one."

"I'll take whatever you've got. Spit it out."

"Well, we know where the road is... or was."

"Yeah, but we can't get to the path beyond the campsites."

"Right, but what if we didn't take a path and just went through the trees?"

"We tried that back at camp. Didn't work so well."

"No. No, it didn't."

Jackie bit at her lower lip. "What about the stream?"

Erik looked in the opposite direction, at the stream which babbled past the sites. The sounds of it had faded into the background, barely noticed. "What's your idea?"

"I wouldn't go so far as to call it an idea."

"Just spit it out Jackie."

"Okay, how's this? The stream passes by and keeps going to who knows where... But it *has* to go somewhere."

"With you so far."

"So, we follow it to whatever body of water it empties into."

"The lake where we did boating."

"That makes sense."

"What's to stop that from looping around?"

"Nothing at all." Jackie sighed. "What's to stop the forest from closing in and preventing us from reaching the road?"

"So either way we're fucked."

"Better than just sitting here."

"Not by much."

"Which way? Road or stream? And don't you dare suggest splitting up."

"I wasn't about to." Erik weighed the options. Much as he hated to admit it the water held more promise. "We tried the trees earlier, let's try your stream."

Jackie got to her feet, exhaustion starting to grab at her. "I'm not used to this much physical activity anymore. How did we do it?"

"We were kids with limitless energy."

She followed him across the campsite. The trees were thinner here, with semi-worn paths leading to the stream. On picnic days and campouts the kids would wade in up to their ankles and splash around.

Good times.

Better times than anything Erik had before or since for sure.

So why hadn't he appreciated it more back then?

Their lights showed the slow-moving water, rippling over stones, the movement of water carrying to their ears. In the center was a wide clear spot where all stones and bigger rocks had been removed to make it safer for kids.

"You think we should cross the stream?" Erik asked.

Jackie considered and shook her head. "Cold, wet feet won't be pleasant if we're here all night. Let's see how this side works out."

Erik started to follow the water downstream.

From the corner of his eye a shadow moved separate from the others. He pointed the flashlight in that direction.

Nothing there.

"What is it?" Jackie said.

Hungry a voice whispered on the breeze.

It came from behind them.

CHAPTER

NINETEEN

Blood from Rob's heart coursed down Ben's hand and arm to spatter against the floor in a dripping *pat-pat-pat* sound. A coppery scent filled the room. Ben looked at it with fascination, turning the gory item left and right.

His smile widened.

This thing had told Miles and Nick to run and that was what they did. Out the door and down the steps.

"What the fuck was that?" Nick asked.

"Don't know."

"Jesus, fuck! Rob!"

Nick came to a stop and turned, looking like he was about to go back in.

Miles grabbed one arm. "Rob is past helping."

A glance at his feet, a shake of his head. "Which way?"

Miles stood in the path trying to look in every direction

at once. Usually confident in his actions and able to make quick decisions, the sensation of total uncertainty overwhelmed him.

"I..."

Nick looked over his shoulder. There was movement in the cottage. "Okay, this way."

Nick reasoned that returning to camp just put them back in the same position so anywhere but that had to be a good move. There was still no working phone, there were no weapons to defend themselves, and worst of all, there was no escape. If they kept heading up this road then they could get to other cottages, maybe follow this road past everything and down the other side.

Did the road continue?

Nick couldn't remember, besides things change. Things change. All he knew for sure was he didn't want either of them to end up like Rob.

"This way," he repeated.

The two took off at a sprint up the road, dark trees lined either side, no cottages for a while. Miles looked over one shoulder.

"Nothing following," he said. "Not yet."

Ben's cottage was left behind as they continued to sprint side by side.

"That wasn't Ben," Miles said between huffs of breath.

Nick shook his head. It had looked like Ben, sounded like him... but no, unless something had given their friend incredible strength and driven him insane then that couldn't have been Ben.

"What was it?"

"I don't know."

The path ahead was clear and straight for several yards, if they could keep up the pace then just maybe they could leave that Ben-thing in the dust.

"Maybe—" Miles began.

The two were sprinting at their best speed when they slammed into an invisible wall. One moment they were running and the next they'd come to a bone-jarring halt, feeling as if they'd run full-tilt into a brick wall.

Nick's hands were ahead of him, flashlight leading the way, and both took the brunt of the impact. The flashlight shattered, driving bits of cheap plastic into his hands. It pulled a scream from his throat. Miles had been running head down, like a sprinter, arms pumping. Head and neck took the full impact as his still moving body drove him into the barrier. Both fell to the dirt road where Nick writhed in agony, trying to pull bits of plastic from his hand. Miles lay dazed, eyes unfocussed, fighting unconsciousness.

"Fuck!" Nick hissed against the pain. "Fuck, fuck, fuck!"

Miles got one hand under him, pushing himself up then collapsed against it, face against the ground, gurgling.

"Shit, Miles, are you okay?"

Stupid question, but the thing you always said when you knew someone wasn't in the neighbourhood of okay. Nick had no idea what to do for his friend. Miles could be out cold for hours. Shit, he may have broken his neck or gotten a concussion.

"What can I fucking do here?"

Nothing.

Miles outweighed him by fifty pounds or more. Carrying his friend back to camp was impossible. He wouldn't even be able to drag him.

Nick looked back the way they'd come.

The road was empty. No thing wearing Ben's face... was that the source of their problems, or just a symptom?

Placing his injured hand against one leg Nick reached out and touched the barrier before him. As far as he could see there was nothing there. Just the cool night air, but his palm pressed up tight against something. It sent a ripple of revulsion through him, like he'd place his hand into a nest of cockroaches. His heart beat stronger inside his ears until he pulled the hand back.

Just beyond the barrier were more cottages.

Could he go around?

Nick dragged himself onto his feet while Miles groaned, face pressed to the dirt and dust. Forcing one hand up tight against the barrier Nick traced it along to the right until he reached an impassible point where trees began. Knowing the result already he travelled in the other direction, once again reaching an end. He suspected that even if he could get around the trees and bushes that this wall continued on anyway.

Another groan.

Nick bent and pressed his good hand up against Miles's back.

"Hey, Miles. You with me?"

Groan.

"We gotta get moving."

"Uh-huh."

Miles rolled over to reveal his face. Blood ran freely down from a nose with an unnatural twist to it. The right side of his face was red and inflamed, the eye already swelling shut.

"Hurts." Was all Miles managed.

He'd lost a front tooth as well.

"We gotta go man. This is a dead end."

Miles opened his unswollen eye and looked left and right, like a trapped animal. "Yeah, 'kay. Help me up."

He grabbed Miles, pulling him upward until the bigger man stood under his own power, swaying. Nick scooped up Miles's flashlight from the road and pointed it back the way they'd come. Once again there was only darkness. They staggered forward like soldiers after a battle, lucky to have survived.

Step by step, foot by foot, they followed the path leading back to camp. Their sole flashlight lit the way, revealing the next foot as the last was left behind.

Step.

Step.

Step.

Movement in the darkness.

A sound from behind.

Nick swung the flashlight around. The road behind was empty.

"Something's following us," Miles said.

"I heard it."

"Fuck."

"Let's hurry."

"Yeah, but I don't want to sprint into another... whatever that was."

"Good point."

They turned back, the flashlight landing on the thing that looked like Ben.

He stood in the middle of the road, blocking their path.

"You should have headed back to camp."

CHAPTER

TWENTY

Patrick stood in the office, looking to the door, then the back hallway, back to the useless radio. He felt as if he were spinning in circles, one foot nailed to the floor. Should he just wait for the half hour to be up and everyone to return?

What if no one *came* back?

Like Gillian.

The radio had been a bust, but one of the others would have an idea how to use it.

Lisa would know.

Lisa should have been there already.

In a blink Patrick was out the door and crossing the upper compound, flashlight sweeping left and right. One ear out for the giggles of the mad cook. His mind struggled to convince him that had all been imagination.

"Were's Gillian then?"

On that his mind was stubbornly quiet.

He knew he was placing a lot of hope on Lisa knowing how to use the radio, but she'd always been the smarter one in the group. There was a possibility she would know how something worked. Convinced he rushed forward to the cabin and through the open door, stopping with one foot just inside.

"Noooo," he half wailed, bringing his hands up to pull at his hair. "No, no, no."

The cabin was a shambles, their belongings thrown everywhere. Suitcases had been opened and contents ransacked. Backpacks had been shredded.

And the blood!

"Lisa?" he called, knowing there was nowhere for her to be hiding. He tried again anyway. "Lisa?"

The amount of destruction and blood told him everything he needed to know. Lisa was gone. Not knowing why, he stepped deeper into the cabin, acutely aware of three things: He was alone, he had no weapon, and he should just get the hell out of there.

"We should have never split up."

Flashlight left, then right. Sure someone was creeping up behind him.

Was this all the crazy cook's doing?

It seemed different.

The blood was centralized on one side, starting near Lisa's bed and continuing underneath.

"Aw, Lisa."

With a groan he got down on one knee and shoved the flashlight toward the underside of the bed, ready to see Lisa's lifeless body.

It was empty. No Lisa.

Where was she?

And once again he was aware of how alone he was. Whoever had done this wouldn't stop at one victim.

"Time to go."

He started backing toward the door.

Outside the cabin came the unmistakeable sound of a footstep.

Interlude 5 – 20 Years Ago – The Wendigo

"The counsellor and his kids had gotten lost, taken what he thought was a shortcut from the lake back to camp."

Theo was winging it again, making the story up as he went. He wasn't entirely sure what the subject of this story was going to be. Not yet.

"The counsellor, Rob,"

And here all the kids sitting engrossed with Theo's words turned toward their counsellor who sat off to the side. Rob glanced back and gave his lopsided grin which basically asked: where is this story going? He focussed on the kids.

"Must be another Rob."

Theo cleared his throat and all attention returned to him.

"Anyway, Rob insisted he knew where they were, and that they would come out soon on the road near camp. Even his kids could tell he didn't believe a word of what he was saying."

Theo paused and took a drink of water before continuing. Let the tension build a little, let them feel what it might be like to be lost in a place unfamiliar to them. He was getting an idea of where they would end up too, but not what might happen there.

"Rob stumbled out into the old graveyard a couple of steps ahead of his kids. The old gravestones with their worn away names and dates stood all around reaching for the sky at different angles. Rob had been there once before, the previous summer. He hadn't returned. The place creeped him out."

Another pause. The kids all knew about the old grave-yard though no counsellor had taken their campers there.

"Did they leave?" Jaspal asked.

"Well, they would have," Theo said. "They would have turned right around and gone back to camp the long way except..."

"Except what?" Heath breathed.

"Except when Rob counted his campers, one was missing."

A brief gasp from the kids. A groan from Heath. Jaspal leaned forward, a grin on his face. The twins, Gary and Randy too.

"*Martin!* Rob called, *where are you?*

The others looked around wondering where their cabin mate had gone. It was weird, creepy that he should go missing here.

Who saw him last? Rob demanded.

One boy, Tony, raised his hand and said Martin had been next to him a minute ago."

Theo lunged toward his audience *"Rah!"*

Everyone jumped, even Rob and Miles.

"The shout came from behind a wide tombstone as Martin jumped out toward them. Scaring everyone, even the brave counsellor."

Theo glanced at Rob who covertly flipped him off.

"The kids all laughed but not Rob. He was already annoyed at being lost."

"What did he do?" Heath asked.

"Not much he could do, was there?"

The kids all nodded. They knew very well that counsellors were not allowed to lay a hand on them, as much as some might like to at some points, not unless that kid was posing some sort of danger.

"*Come on, let's get back*, Rob told the kids.

They all agreed this was a good idea. It was getting close to lunch and they were all hungry.

Hungry! A voice agreed from somewhere nearby. Behind them, toward the back of the graveyard.

Rob and the kids froze looking around. He did a quick count and found all accounted for, even that little creep Martin. No one had snuck off to throw another scare into them."

"Who said that?" Gary asked.

"Well..." Theo had latched onto a creature he'd recently read about. "There is a creature called a Wendigo that follows people through the woods."

"Creature?" Heath asked.

"An old native legend. A hunger monster."

"Hunger monster?" Randy said. "What's that?"

Theo was losing them. He'd spent too much time on questions instead of the story. He needed to fix that and ignored Randy's question.

"Rob and the kids all huddled together looking around them for anyone who could have spoken.

Hungry, the voice repeated in a creaky voice like the steps of a haunted house.

It came from behind them again, only now behind them was back toward the only exit. When they spun around again the voice said *Hungry*, once more from behind. It was moving, always just out of sight, always at their backs."

"They should make a circle," Heath said. "Look in all directions."

Jaspal rolled his eyes. Gary chuckled and shook his head. Poor Heath never could come out on top. Theo grinned.

"A great idea, Heath. Unfortunately, Rob and his campers weren't thinking straight by this point. Too bad, that might have worked."

"What happened?" Jaspal asked.

"Rob told the kids they were leaving and started to hustle them toward the path again."

Hunnnnngry! This time the voice came from their right where no one was looking.

What do you want? Rob said.

One, the voice said. *Which one?*

Leave them alone! Rob shouted. He stood with arms out in a guarding position.

Hunnnngryyyyyyyy!!!

Move! Rob ordered, turning to look at them. *Now!*

The kids didn't need extra urging. They rushed forward, past the last of the tombstones and out of the graveyard, onto the path leading beyond. They ran as fast as possible, bumping each other in their panic. Martin fell, tripped by a careless foot that sent him sprawling, scraping the palms of his hands and both knees. The others kept going, out into the sunlight and not stopping until their fear had burned away. They came to a stop, looking around.

The voice had gone, left behind in the graveyard.

Where's Martin? Albert asked.

And Rob? Tony added.

"Ohhhh," Jaspal breathed, seeing what was coming. He

looked to the other kids for confirmation but saw only confusion. To his credit he didn't say a word.

"The kids all gathered, waiting for someone else to go look.

Rob? Albert called.

No answer.

At that moment on the path Martin had rolled over and looked back into the graveyard. What he saw made him jump to his feet and run. He came out of that little path like a rocket and passed his cabin mates. They all followed, trying to keep up. Somehow Martin followed some inner sense that brought them all sprinting into camp.

"What did he see?" Heath asked.

"No one knows. He said nothing while running back, only wearing a look of absolute terror on his face. Martin never spoke another word. Not that day. Not when his parents came to pick him up early. Not even when safe at home. Anytime they tried to ask him questions he just closed his eyes and screamed."

"And Rob?"

"Rob?" Theo looked at his friend with the same name. "Rob never returned to camp. He was never seen again."

CHAPTER

TWENTY-ONE

"Sabrina, be careful," Abby whispered.

Abby wasn't sure if she wanted Sabrina to be careful for her safety, or simply so that she didn't alert whoever had slammed the door that they were upstairs.

She'd forgotten how little she liked that woman.

Abby stood just outside of the corpse-filled room as Sabrina crept toward the top of the stairs. After a moments hesitation Theo followed. Abby made a gurgled sound of barely restrained horror. She knew she wanted Theo to be safe.

The two arrived at the railing which separated them from the area below. The set of stairs came in a straight line, then a landing partway up turned the climber around in a half-circle. For the beginning of that climb anyone coming up would be unaware they were being watched.

They waited in silence.

"One of our friends?" Theo whispered close to Sabrina's ear.

She shook her head.

No. It wouldn't be.

Any of their friends would have called out, especially if they accidentally slammed the door open.

The sound of movement through the downstairs worked its way upward. Someone moving steadily forward.

There was a second sound too.

Something being scraped across the floor, metal on hardwood.

Something with some weight. And it was moving toward the stairs.

Moonlight streamed in through the uncovered window below and painted the downstairs in weak light. A person's shadow played across the steps leading up.

Scrape. Scrape. Scrape.

The shadow came closer to the stairs, followed by the body that created it. A person stepped onto the first of the stairs. Tall, over six feet, and wide in the shoulders. They wore some sort of overalls with no shirt underneath. The head was bald as an egg with a jagged scar that started at the front left and crossed in a lightning bolt to the back right.

"No," Theo whispered. "Can't be."

"What?"

"Luthor. The axe-man."

"From your story?"

CLUNK!

The sound of something hitting against the stair's riser as he climbed to the second floor. Another step up.

CLUNK!

They could see it now. A long gleaming double-bladed axe.

Theo knew then that this was his axe-man. When he'd told that story he hadn't known a lumberjack's axe from a fire fighter's, so he'd given Luthor a double bladed one like a Viking might have carried into battle.

CLUNK!

Theo backed away from the horror coming toward them.

Now they knew what had happened to Doris and her husband.

Sabrina followed and as they retreated one stepped on the wrong spot, a long creaking noise filled the upstairs hall-way. Both froze and spun toward the axe-man.

Luthor turned and looked toward them.

And he smiled.

His eyes were almost comically large and the mouth was crooked but filled with the most perfect teeth. He pursed his lips and whistled a tune as he continued to climb the stairs. Unhurried.

CLUNK!

CLUNK!

CLUNK!

Sabrina and Theo turned and ran back along the hall.

"What is it?" Abby asked. "What did you see?"

"Get in there!" Sabrina ordered.

Abby looked into the gore-filled room and made a whimpering sound, but didn't take a step. When Sabrina reached her, she pushed Abby through the doorway.

"Hey!"

"Stay out there if you want," Sabrina hissed. "Just get out of my way."

Abby looked back toward the hall as Theo rushed in. "What's going on? Who's there?"

"The axe-man," Theo answered.

"Who?"

"From his story," Sabrina explained.

Theo turned and slammed the door shut, looking for a lock.

Nothing.

"Shit!" He spat out. He grabbed the chair in the corner and jammed it under the doorknob.

"That should slow him."

"Slow?" Abby said, fear taking over her voice. "Slow??"

Theo nodded and joined Sabrina who had rushed to the window.

"How is the axe-man here?" Abby demanded. "How is he real?"

"I don't know."

"You made him up, didn't you?"

Theo nodded. "He was some rip off idea from slasher movies. Not exactly original."

"How—?"

"We don't know, Abby," Sabrina turned and said. "Okay? And it doesn't really matter *how* right now or why or anything other than how the fuck do we get out of here."

"But—"

"Either help or shut up."

Once again Abby shut her mouth under Sabrina's tirade.

"Can we get out there?" Theo asked.

"Maybe."

Sabrina grabbed the handles and slid the window up along its track. Then she poked her head out and grabbed something.

"There's a trellis."

"A what?" Abby asked, forgetting to keep her mouth shut.

Sabrina returned to the room. "One of those things for vines or whatever to climb."

"Is it strong enough to hold us?" Theo asked.

"Almost certainly not," Sabrina said. "Do we have a choice?"

Abby rushed to the window and was out before either of the other two could say a word. They squeezed their heads through to watch her making way down slowly and methodically.

"That will never hold more than one of us," Theo said.

Something heavy slammed against the door and the two spun toward it. A second later a follow up impact hit the door and the axe blade penetrated the wood. It was pulled back and another impact came, widening the hole to a point where the axe-man's whistling face could be seen.

"No choice," Theo said. "Go."

Sabrina didn't argue. She crawled out and grabbed onto the trellis. One step down. Two. The increased weight was too much and the entire thing came loose from the house, tilting forward and speeding toward the ground. Abby hit first, the bottom part of the trellis landing on top of her. Sabrina fell in a greater arc and slammed against the ground farther out from the house, rolling to a stop several feet further. She lay unmoving.

Theo turned to see the axe splinter the door panel. Luthor the axe-man reached through, grabbing at the chair that blocked him.

There was no fighting this monster. Theo crawled out through the window.

"No choice," Theo echoed Sabrina's words.

Without a trellis to climb all he could do was hang from the window sill and look for other options.

The noise of the chair being thrown aside reached him.

An old satellite dish jutted from the side of the house a couple of feet down. Too far to grab.

Sound above alerted Theo just in time. The axe bit into the window sill where his fingers had been a moment earlier. Theo had let go already.

Gravity took him.

CHAPTER

TWENTY-TWO

"Something's moving, Erik."

"I see it."

Only he didn't. He saw the spot where it *had* been.

"Where did it go?"

Hungry!

The voice came from behind them. Both Jackie and Erik spun around, sure that whatever it was, it would be close enough to touch. The clearing was empty though.

"What is it?" Jackie asked.

"How the hell would I know?"

"Yeah. No. Right."

Jackie started to back away from the voice, back toward the stream. A moment later Erik moved to join her.

Hungry!

Once again it came from behind them. Once again they turned to find nothing.

"It's following us."

Erik shook his head. "No, it's circling us."

"So we both agree it's an *it,* and not a who."

Erik had no response to that.

"Where do we go?" Jackie asked.

"I don't know."

Where did you go when something stalked you from all sides?

Was it all sides though?

"It's always behind us," he said.

"Yeah."

"Turn away from the stream."

They turned in unison. Once again the voice came from behind.

Which one?

"Let's go!" Erik said. "Fast! And do *not* look back."

He took Jackie's hand and they rushed forward, toward the campsite again.

"Where do we go?" Jackie asked.

"The other idea. Into the trees, toward the road."

"Yeah. Yeah, okay."

The two kept a quick pace while around them the shadows were alive with movement, just out of the corners of their eyes. They neared the trees which would hopefully lead to... anywhere but here.

Which one? The voice repeated, right at their ears, just a step back.

Jackie jumped, jerking around to look back.

"No!" Erik shouted.

Too late. Jackie stumbled, dragging Erik's attention around as well as he struggled to keep them both upright.

"What do you want?" Jackie screamed.

Hungry! The voice said from the trees behind them, exactly where they wanted to go.

Both Erik and Jackie felt an impact, a hard shove that bordered on a punch. It took them in the center of their backs and threw them forward. Both flashlights went flying in different directions as they sprawled into the dirt. Jackie's hit the rocks, the glass protective lens and bulb beyond shattering. Erik's hit the ground and rolled, hitting a rock that sent it into a spin. When it came to rest the light faced away from them.

"No!" Erik yelled, flipping onto his back.

Around them, without the benefit of flashlights, the shadows were deep and dark and moving. A living darkness, separate from those made by the trees. It towered above them, seven feet at least. Gleaming eyes and teeth.

Jackie struggled to roll over.

"Nuh... nuh... nuh..." was all she could manage.

Erik tried to back-pedal while struggling to see whatever stalked them. It came closer. Closer.

Food, the voice whispered next to their ears.

"Food?" Jackie said. "We have no food."

Which one?

"Oh fuck!" Erik groaned. "No, please."

Jackie just shook her head moaning over and over, "No, no, no."

Those terrible eyes, hunkered down at their feet. It scrabbled closer until they could see it more clearly.

They wished they couldn't.

It was thin to the point of emaciation. If it had been human it would have starved before now. It leaned forward, the meagre moonlight catching its yellowish eyes, its gleaming, sharp teeth.

Erik whimpered as he tried to retreat more.

"Please," he said.

"It's not going to listen, Erik."

"No. No... I... "

Which one? The monster repeated.

Erik glanced at Jackie then back at the monster. "Her! Take her!"

"What?! You bastard!" she screamed. "No, take—"

The monster fell on Jackie, all teeth and claws as Erik back-pedaled away.

Her screams chased him as he got to his feet and fled.

CHAPTER

TWENTY-THREE

Trapped.

Miles and Nick stood still, staring toward the thing that looked like Ben, evaluating their options. The Ben-thing didn't move any closer, only waiting and blocking their path.

"It can't get both of us," Nick said.

"No."

Neither made a move.

"But... It *will* get one of us," Nick sighed. "Won't it?"

Miles nodded his agreement.

Neither could look at the other. Instead Nick focussed on the monster before them.

"It's been great knowing you," he said and started toward the thing which had killed Rob.

"Don't do it."

"It's going to get one of us."

"Yeah, but... Why you?"

"Why not?" Nick took another step.

Miles's shoulder bumped Nick as he raced past, barrelling toward the Ben monster.

"No! Miles!"

"Go!"

In the last moment before reaching Ben, Miles launched himself into a flying tackle that had him collide with the creature.

"Go!" he yelled again.

Nick raced forward, slowing to stare at the writing mass on the ground.

The Ben thing had gotten the advantage and sat on top of Miles, holding him down.

If they attacked together then surely... Nick rushed forward, ready to aim a kick at the side of its head.

Shoulders grew, widening. Arms lengthened. The monster's mouth dropped into an impossible dark hole, big enough to swallow first a baseball, then a football and still grew more. As it grew the thing howled, a noise that shook Nick to his core.

"No," he shouted, voice quivering. "No!"

Nick stepped forward, preparing to place that intended kick to the side of its head. As he did the Ben-thing shifted focus to him. Now the face was all yawning abyss of mouth. It screamed into his face, and his soul. Nick stopped, tried to reverse and tripped over his own feet, falling into the dirt.

"Hey! Ben!" Miles yelled up at the monster, regaining its attention. He spit into its face. "You always were a pussy!"

The thing screamed into Miles's face.

"Go, Nick! Now!"

Nick went, scrambling to his feet and rushing back the way they'd come. He felt like the guiltiest piece of shit that ever walked the earth. Miles sacrificed himself for him. For *him!!!* He was damned if he would let that go wasted... Or was that just his way to compensate for never placing that kick on the monster's head. God damn it!

Survivor guilt.

Only... he hadn't survived. Not yet.

Just delayed the end.

Nick forced his feet to keep moving, to keep him upright. If he slowed, if he fell, and that thing got him then Miles's sacrifice would be for nothing at all.

And it *was* a sacrifice.

Miles started to scream.

This was a never before heard sound to Nick. Miles had always been one of the toughest guys. Not in some stupid macho way, but in a calm and confident way. Miles always knew what to do and just did it. Not just doing things right, but doing the right thing too.

So was his sacrifice the right thing?

"How the hell am I a better person to survive than Miles?"

Nick didn't even realize he was speaking out loud. He was just trying to distract himself, to drown out the noise.

The screaming.

It continued.

"No. No, no, no, no, no!!!"

Nick wanted to turn back, to help Miles, but his feet just kept moving him forward as fast as they could until he crossed back onto camp property.

Guilt nipped at his heels the entire way.

TWENTY-FOUR

Theo grabbed for the satellite dish arm as he fell, knowing if he missed it, he would fall to the ground and break both legs. Positioned halfway between the window he'd just left and the next one down he hadn't picked up too much speed as he grasped for the dish. Still, grabbing it to stop his fall felt like grabbing a speeding car. The dish itself punched his stomach and drove the breath from him.

"Ooof," he wheezed.

The apparatus held his weight a full second but it had never been meant to take weight. It pulled free with the shriek of steel screws withdrawing from aluminum siding. Theo fell again toward the next window. This one had a sill jutting out to place plants on and he crashed through a tomato plant left there to catch the sun, its owners murdered before it could be brought in for the night. The whole thing wasn't wide enough and Theo, unbalanced, rolled to the right and fell onto the lawn.

One hand under him he struggled to get up, stomach feeling as if he'd taken a punch from Miles. Legs shaky from the landing. He rolled onto his back and looked back the way he'd come.

"How did I survive that?"

Above, Luthor leaned motionless, upper body poking from the window. He stared at Theo, perhaps wondering if he should make the same jump. A moment later he withdrew into the house.

"Move!" Theo wheezed. "Move your ass."

He scrambled to get his feet under him and staggered away from the house. Ten feet distant Abby was trapped under the collapsed trellis, panicking, struggling to get free. Several feet further lay the unmoving lump which was Sabrina. She'd fallen farthest and suffered the worst for it. Theo staggered over to Abby. He grabbed the wooden trellis and lifted. Abby continued to struggle.

"Abby! Just crawl out."

The words penetrated and Abby rolled to one side, getting free and onto her feet. She looked around.

"Where is he? Where?"

Theo looked toward the door they'd entered and shook his head. "He's coming."

"Then let's go."

"Yeah," he rushed to Sabrina and bent over her.

She remained motionless but breathing.

"Leave her. There's no time."

"Leave her?"

Abby was already rushing away, heading back toward the camp. She didn't look back, as if her decision was obvious.

The door behind him slammed.

Theo spun to see Luthor, the axe-man stalking across the lawn toward him. He moved in the steady but unhurried manner of movie maniacs everywhere.

Twenty seconds.

Maybe.

He slapped Sabrina, hard. "Wake up."

A groan. A flutter of eyelids.

Another glance back.

Ten.

Theo grabbed Sabrina by one hand and jerked her upwards. The woman fought to control her feet and continue standing. One arm draped over his shoulder Theo started to get her moving forward. As soon as she had some sort of wits about her again, they could run separately.

Theo began to glance back again, knowing it was a bad idea. This was when people tripped in movies and became easy targets, he'd used it himself in more than one book. He couldn't help himself.

"Sabrina, we have to—"

The impact came from his right and threw them both sideways. Theo rolled on the ground while Sabrina staggered aside holding something.

What the hell was that?

Theo scrambled to get up again, but his legs refused to work.

Sabrina held what looked like an arm.

His arm.

"Fuck!" he said.

Tried to.

His voice deserted him, like the strength in his legs.

He tried to roll but the axe stopped him. It was under his body. The axe-man had dropped it or—

Sabrina screamed.

--or Theo had pulled it from the axe-man's hands when it wedged into his body.

The world around Theo started to go grey.

A few feet away Luthor looked down at his hands as if just realizing something was missing.

"Run!" he whispered.

With the last of his strength.

They were his last words.

Sabrina spun and took off at a sprint, passing Abby as she went without so much as a glance at her.

TWENTY-FIVE

Someone was coming.

"No!" Patrick whispered.

He glanced around for a weapon and found only the flashlight already in his hand.

"That will have to do," he whispered and positioned himself by the door.

He raised the makeshift weapon over his head as the footsteps came closer.

Closer.

Movement just outside and a body came flying through the door. The flashlight was already coming down, aimed at the intruder's head. He realized it was Nick a moment before impact and pulled up, giving him a glancing blow against the shoulder instead.

"Jesus, Pat!"

"Sorry, sorry. It's just..." He gestured at the cabin and stepped aside.

Nick looked around without much surprise.

"Lisa?"

"I assume it's her blood."

Nick nodded, looking sad. "Who else could it be?"

"Where are Rob and Miles?"

A long sigh, bordering on a sob. Nick launched into what they'd seen, the fake Ben who had killed Rob. Miles's sacrifice.

"Both of them? Gone?"

Nick nodded. "What do we do?"

Ben. Gillian. Lisa. Now Rob and Miles.

"What do we do, Pat?"

"I... have no idea. Unless you know how to work the radio in the office."

"No."

"Me either."

"Where's Gillian?"

"Gone. Grabbed from right behind me."

Patrick told the story of them being stalked by the crazy cook and her taking the slowest in the group.

"I could have let her go first, to lead the way with the flashlight."

"You couldn't have known."

"I could if I'd thought of Theo's story."

"Theo's...?"

"It's like it came to life."

Nick nodded. "Yeah. Yeah. The doppelgangers."

"Sounds like maybe what you ran into."

"So, how the hell are his stories alive here?"

"Just the creepy shit he told at night."

"What do you mean?"

"Well, we're not seeing the Fluffies here. Or King Raccoon."

Two characters made up for daytime stories for the kids. Cute and cuddly stuff, not what Theo enjoyed telling at all.

Pat shrugged. "I guess those have been banished by the darker creatures."

"Where is everyone else?"

"I don't know. After what's happened I'm afraid to consider."

"We need Theo," Nick said. "He made the stories up for god's sake. He should know how to fight them."

"Maybe. I don't remember his stories having happy endings."

"That's true."

"Okay, I am feeling really exposed here. Where to?"

Nick looked around, like a solution would jump out. "I don't know, let's take a look at the radio. Maybe we can figure it out together."

Pat looked dubious, but had no better suggestions. The others were supposed to meet back at the office anyway.

The two started across the upper compound feeling incredibly exposed. Each step was a little faster than the last. Then a noise came from the darkness to their right, something moving quick. Both spun, on guard, fight or flight once again grasping at them.

"Nick!" the voice called, "Pat!"

Erik came stumbling from the shadows to almost fall at their feet. He glanced back over his shoulder like a man with all of hell on his heels.

Interlude 6 – 20 Years Ago - Leviticus

THEO LEANED toward the kids around him, not entirely sure what he was going to do for a story. These kids had heard all of his good stuff and he would have to improvise. Problem was that a cold had grabbed him in a fist and his head felt full of cotton.

Summer colds were the worst.

He knew this wouldn't be his best, but he could at least not flat out embarrass himself.

"Everyone knows how the lake is deep, right?"

Nods and murmurs all around. Down at the lake where boating happened, the beach sloped into the water for ten feet before dropping off immediately and drastically. At ten feet the water was up to an adult's waist, then it went straight down thirty feet.

Deep. Dark. Mysterious.

To one side Gillian sat with arms crossed. She was here under protest and had been convinced to allow her cabin a chance to hear a spooky story. Next to her was Patrick, the only one who could have convinced her. Abby's cabin was there too.

"What lives under that water? You ever wonder?"

The kids looked to each other, shrugs all around. No one had ever thought about it until now. Even so, under the water was a different world, and one which was generally avoided.

So what *did* live down there? He asked himself.

"Have any of you seen any fish?"

Thoughtful expressions. Shakes of the head.

It was something he'd noticed himself.

The fish must be deeper down.

"There's no fish, because Leviticus has eaten them all."

"Leviticus?" One boy asked.

"The lake monster."

"Ooh," Mary-Louise said.

Sarah leaned forward too.

He'd never been so grateful for those two kids. They'd asked for him tonight.

He felt his forehead. It was hot. Feverish. He should be in bed, but a request was a request. Had to keep the fans happy.

"Leviticus has lived down there since cavemen wandered the wilderness. He's eaten everything he can down there and grown big because of it.

"Why doesn't he starve then?" one kid asked. Chris?

"Well, because every spring the locals bring in a truck full of fish and dump it in the lake to keep Leviticus happy."

Yeah, that worked. He had an idea.

"But every once in a while... they forget. Or someone decides that Leviticus isn't real."

"Then what happens," a boy, Charlie, from Pat's cabin asked.

"Then Leviticus gets hungry."

A shudder went through the room.

"Last year was one of those years. They didn't re-stock the lake and one of our counsellors disappeared."

"I was here last year," a kid names Nathalie said. "I don't remember that."

Aw, crap. He'd missed that little detail.

Damn fever!

"Well, we don't let the campers know, of course..."

Nathalie looked dubious. Theo was losing her and that sort of thing was infectious.

"Anderson," Gillian said.

Theo looked at his friend, feeling the fever sweat coursing down his face. For a moment he had no idea what she was talking about then it clicked and Theo smiled. Every year there's someone who comes to camp and it just isn't for them. They last a week at most, usually less, and then just leave. It can be a hard job mentally and emotionally.

Anderson.

"He was a first-year counsellor last year. He came up here with the rest of us and then one night he went down to the lake for a swim and never came back."

Nathalie considered that. "Yeah. Yeah! I remember him. Tall guy."

"That's the one."

Her expression changed from doubtful to convinced and Theo breathed a sigh of relief.

He could have kissed Gillian.

Time to wrap this up.

"Leviticus stays low when the sun is hot, but at night when things cool down...? Well, let's just say you won't catch me skinny dipping out there at night."

With that he gave a wink and looked around.

Gillian's arms were no longer crossed and she gave him a brief nod of congratulations. He smiled back at her and gathered himself to leave. He needed aspirin and a good night's sleep.

TWENTY-SIX

"Erik!" Nick cried.

Their friend staggered from the shadows toward them and Nick reached out both hands to prevent him from falling flat on his face. Even so Erik went down to one knee, looking back the way he'd come again. Pat grabbed one arm and Nick the other.

"Let's get him inside," Pat said, looking at those surrounding shadows.

"Inside," Erik agreed. "Please."

They crossed the upper compound toward the office, the shadows seeming to follow.

"Huh!" Pat grunted.

"What?"

"The lights are still on."

Nick shrugged, not seeing Patrick's point.

"It's just... Well, whatever trapped us here has prevented our escape, destroyed the phones, and even killed some of us." This last bit was spoken in a lower voice and Pat's voice faltered, distracted. He shook it off. "You would think they'd cut off the electricity too."

"Don't give them ideas," Nick said.

"Yeah," Erik agreed in a lower voice. "Doing okay on their own."

Inside they let Erik sag into the office chair.

"Where's Jackie?" Nick asked, afraid he already knew the answer.

"Gone."

"Gone?" Pat asked.

Erik nodded. "Some kind of thin monster. It was tall and looked starved. It jumped on her. Teeth and claws. It... It..."

"You just left her?" Nick asked.

Erik looked up into his face, then Pat's, a bit of his old defiance in his eyes. Still, he looked aside before answering. "Yeah, I did."

Neither man said anything further about it.

"We were stuck in a loop."

"A loop?" Nick said.

"It was..." He took a deep breath and let it loose. "We were trying to get out through the camp sites, to get to the road."

"We remember," Nick said.

"We got to the first site, but each time we went down the path we just came back to the same one. Over and over."

"Did you try going back?" Nick asked.

"Gee, I guess we never thought about that," Erik rolled his eyes. "For fuck's sake. Yes, we tried that and it was the same. We tried to get to the stream and that's when this monster came out of the shadows."

"The Wendigo," Nick said.

"Huh?"

"Did it stay just outside of your vision? When you turned it was somewhere else?"

"Yeah. Yeah! For a while anyway, until it attacked us… from behind." He looked at his hands as if just discovering they were empty. "I dropped my flashlight."

Arms crossed, Nick asked. "How did you get out of the loop?"

"It… I ran, when it got Jackie, you know."

Nick scoffed. Patrick nodded.

"And it let me go. I stumbled out at the pool and didn't stop running until I saw you."

"Brave guy," Nick said.

"Hey, fuck you man! You weren't there."

Nick stared a moment longer then looked away, remembering the fact that he too had run while a friend died. Difference was that Miles told him to go.

"It was like… I don't know," Erik muttered. "Like it got what it wanted and I was dismissed."

A sacrifice.

"The Wendigo," Nick said, ignoring Erik to focus on Pat. "Another of Theo's stories."

"Theo?" Erik asked. "What do you mean?"

Pat explained how he and Gillian had been stalked by the crazy cook and how she'd disappeared. Nick followed up with what had happened to Miles and Rob, and how Ben had attacked them.

"Only it wasn't Ben. It was something that looked like Ben."

"Shit!" Erik said, nodding. "You think Theo has something to do with this?"

"I..." Pat looked to Nick. "It never occurred to me. Maybe."

"And he's off with Sabrina and Abby?"

Pat glanced to the door and back again. None of them made a move toward looking for the remaining group.

"What about Lisa?"

"I went to our cabin and it was torn apart. There was blood everywhere."

The three remained in silence a moment before Erik broke it again. "So, why are we here?"

"This is the meetup point," Nick explained. "Everyone is supposed to come back here after half an hour..."

Nick trailed off, seeing just how much had happened in that time. A glance at his watch told him they were over that half hour now. Was this it? The three of them?

"Gillian and I found the radio, before she disappeared but I have no idea what I'm doing. Any chance you know how to use it?"

"Yeah, maybe. I played around with it a bit back then."

Nick and Pat both brightened.

For the first time they had some vague hope.

Pat turned, looking toward where he'd left the radio, sure that it would be gone now, but it still sat on the desk, waiting. Would it be destroyed inside? Would the power go out?

Something would happen.

Erik made his way across the entry to the radio and sat

before it. He moved a little more easily now that he'd had a chance to rest. First he turned it around, made a couple of adjustments to how it was hooked up, then flipped a switch. A light came on and the radio hummed.

"You almost had it," he said.

Pat nodded, grateful for the out of character positive comment.

"Of course, close is only good in horseshoes," Erik added, "and hand grenades."

That was more expected.

Erik turned the dial and moved through static, landing on a clear spot. He picked up the microphone and depressed the switch on the side.

"Anyone out there?"

Erik let go of the button and waited.

"Aren't you supposed to say *over* or something?" Nick asked.

"Ten-four good buddy," Erik said. "That sort of shit?"

Nick shrugged and Erik depressed the button again.

"Breaker-breaker, anyone got their ears on out there?"

No response.

Erik turned to Nick and held out the microphone. "You want to try?"

"You're doing fine." Nick stepped back and sat in the chair that Erik had vacated.

"Try another channel," Pat suggested.

"Sure thing boss."

Erik spun the dial some more until landing on another static-free spot.

"Camp White Bear calling anyone out there," he said then released the button.

A crackling came from the radio. Faint.

"I hear you White Bear."

Nick was up again, coming to stand by Patrick.

"Tell them we have an emergency here," Patrick said. "Tell them someone is hurt."

Erik held the microphone out to Pat who looked at it a moment then took it. They exchanged spots.

"We're at the camp," Pat said.

Erik scoffed. "He already knows that. Don't waste time."

A scowl from Pat but he nodded.

"Someone is hurt here. We need help."

A crackle of static.

A giggle.

THUNK!

THUNK!

THUNK!

"What the hell is that?" Nick asked.

"That giggle," Pat said. "I think that was the old crazy cook."

HUNGRY

Erik stepped back. "No. No, no. That was the thing that got Jackie."

Join us. A voice hissed from the speaker. Low. Sibilant. Like a snake. *Come to us.*

Stay where you are. A different voice came from the radio. Strong and demanding. *We'll come get you.*

Somewhere nearby a scream filled the air and then was gone.

"What the hell was that?" Erik said.

"Abby, I think," Nick said with a shrug. "Maybe Sabrina?"

TWENTY-SEVEN

The three turned toward the door.

Shallow, mocking laughter came from the radio's speaker, filling the office.

Patrick spun the dial away, the laughter following them through the entire range of frequencies.

Whooooo's nexxxxxttttt?

He jumped from the chair as if the voice could reach through and grab him, almost tipping the whole thing in the process. Erik rushed forward and snapped the power off.

Come out and play!

Nick got down on his knees and unplugged the radio. Only then did it fall silent, and only as an unnerving slow fade. The three stood looking at each other then to the radio.

"That means..." Patrick began, reasoning things through the panic that wanted to engulf him. "That means we *can't* communicate with the outside world."

Erik turned. "How do you figure?"

"If we could, they would have taken the radio while I was in the cabin."

"They?" Erik asked. "Who are they?"

"The mad cook," Nick said. "The doppelganger. The wendigo."

"No," Erik shook his head. "None of those."

"What?"

"Those are all... I don't know. Minions? Monsters? None of them are the mastermind."

"No, you're right." Patrick turned to him. "They're just the ones speaking."

"Does that knowledge help us at all?" Nick asked.

Erik shrugged.

"Not yet," Pat admitted.

"Great."

"Are we it then?" Erik asked, getting back on his feet. "The survivors?"

"I don't know," Pat admitted.

"Who are we sure of?" Nick asked.

"Jackie, Gillian, Lisa, Miles, Rob. Ben."

"Fuck," Erik muttered. "Half of us."

"Don't know about Theo, Sabrina and Abby," Nick pointed out. "Or the cook and her husband too."

"Yeah?" Erik said. "Maybe they're behind it all."

"What, they cast some kind of kitchen spell?" Nick asked. "Made the trees grow?"

Patrick shrugged. "I'm not discounting anything at this point."

"Whatever," Erik sighed. "The important question is what do we do?"

Both men looked to Pat.

"I think... maybe we survive to morning?"

"Oh yeah? Why morning?"

"If this is like a movie then there has to be a way out, a way to survive."

"Pretty thin reasoning," Erik said.

"It is."

"It's all we've got though," Nick added. "Right?"

Erik sighed and looked around. "If we're going to make it to morning then we'd better barricade this office."

"And take turns on watch," Nick added.

It was something to do, a way to have some control or at least feel like they did, however slim it was. There were two doors. The front one which was main entry, and a lesser used back door on the far end of the office. Usually that would bring them to the parked cars but right now...

"I'll make sure that back door is secure," Erik said and started toward the hallway.

The sound of pounding feet on the stairs brought all three men around to face the front door. Fists were clenched, raised.

Instead of the expected monster Sabrina barged through looking like she'd survived a battle. A moment later Abby followed. Both women were scratched and bruised. Sabrina looked like she would have a black eye by morning. Abby slammed the door shut behind them and looked around.

"Sabrina!" Pat said. "Abby!"

"Thanks a lot for waiting for me," Abby said to Sabrina.

Sabrina ignored her, saying to the room: "Someone help

me move the desk." She grabbed one side and saw no one moved to help. "Come on!"

"What are you doing?" Nick asked, grabbing a side.

"Barricading the door," Sabrina explained.

"Why—?" Pat began.

"The axe-man!" Abby exploded, half scream, half sob.

"The axe-man?" Pat said.

"Fuck," Erik added. "I forgot about him."

"That's four of Theo's stories come to life," Nick said, sliding the desk into place.

"Four?" Sabrina said.

"Where's Theo?" Pat asked.

Abby shook her head.

Sabrina said. "Axe-man got him."

"Shit!" Erik hissed.

"We could have used his knowledge," Pat said.

"Knowledge," Sabrina asked, "what knowledge?"

"His stories," Nick explained. "We've encountered the crazy cook, the doppelganger, the Wendigo, and now the axe-man."

Abby looked around. "Is this everyone?"

Nick placed a hand on her shoulder and felt her flinch under it. "Afraid so."

"Haven't seen a body for Gillian, Lisa or Ben," Nick said hopefully.

Erik flinched at the mention of Ben, remembering how he'd left because of Erik's teasing. Had he been the first victim? Had the doppelganger gotten him? That was how the story worked. The creature needed to kill the original to take their place.

"I think we can assume the worst," Erik said.

Abby went to the shelf and grabbed the remaining flashlight, the one meant for Ben.

"What's the plan?" Sabrina asked.

"What you're already doing," Pat explained. "Barricade ourselves in. Wait for morning."

Sabrina looked at the desk in front of the door. "That's the best we have?"

"Unless you have a better idea," Patrick said.

She shook her head. "I'll go secure the back door."

"You shouldn't go alone," Pat replied. "Nick?"

Sabrina turned back. "I'll go alone thanks. Group work didn't do us much good."

She glared at Abby then turned and headed down the hall, not waiting for an answer. Everyone glanced around, remembering their lost friends, unable to meet each other's eyes.

"Cheerful thoughts," Erik said.

TWENTY-EIGHT

Sabrina left the small entry, headed for the back door. She was glad the power was on, having lost her flashlight back in the fall from the trellis. Her back and side hurt and she wondered if there wasn't a broken rib. There was no time for pain though.

This back room was one spot most of them had never seen much of while working here. No one really came into the office of the camp director unless they were being fired. It was one longish hallway—long for a camp full of one room cabins anyway—with doors on the left-hand side. The first one stood open and Sabrina poked her head inside, flipped the light switch. A small bathroom. Next was a storage room filled with file boxes and some cabinets. Archaic. It should all be digitized if they really wanted to keep it.

The next room was Gillian's office. Gillian. The one who had convinced her to come back here today. Sabrina shook her head, gritted her teeth. How had she done it?

Sabrina had been prepared to tell them all to fuck off, that part of her life was dead and in the past, but Gillian reminded her of good times and the carefree days of youth.

No one to blame but herself.

Now Gillian was gone and Sabrina had no intention of joining her.

She shook her head and kept moving. One more door. This one closed and at the end of the hallway which she guessed would lead to a small back entrance. She gripped the knob and pushed it into the room ahead of her. Expecting... well, she really wasn't sure what to expect.

She looked around the small room. Off to one side was an aging photocopier and a short counter to the other. Something moved beside the counter. Her fists came up in a defensive motion, pulling at her wounded side and drawing a gasp of pain.

Fight past it. She was ready for anything. Between fight and flight, she was always in fight mode.

All she could see from this angle were a pair of white running shoes pressed flat against the floor, unmoving. "Come out of there."

No response. The shoes pulled in a little.

Should she get one of the others?

Fuck that!

Sabrina inched closer, heart pounding. She traced an arc to the left, trying to see more of who was hunkered down beside the counter.

"Gillian?"

No, not Gillian. Sabrina could see dark hair instead of

sandy blonde. The head was down, hiding the person's face. A larger body shape than Gillian's.

"Lisa?"

The other woman looked up. Her face was red and puffy from crying. Swelling had started on the right side of her face where she'd taken some sort of hit. There was dried blood in her hair, trailing from one side down to her chin. The eye there was well on its way to swelling shut.

A matching set with Sabrina's.

Lisa said no words, just stared back.

"Lisa, it's me. It's Sabrina."

The unswollen eye fixed on Sabrina, staring.

Sabrina cursed inwardly. She *should* have gotten one of the others. She was the last person to be soft and nurturing, which is what Lisa needed. Too late now.

"What happened?" Sabrina tried.

Lisa's good eye jerked left and she tried to backpedal away. Sabrina realized those were the exact wrong words.

Fuck's sake!

"It's okay. It's just me." Sabrina held up both hands, showing she held nothing threatening. "The others are in the front office."

The unswollen eye widened.

Sabrina nodded. "Patrick, Nick, Erik and Abby."

A grunt. Eyes widened but no other attempt to retreat. Something about that group was okay, but there was a question in that face,

"That's everyone. Sorry."

The tension left Lisa's body. There was someone she hoped *not* to see.

"You're safe." Sabrina gritted her teeth against that obvious lie and shook her head. She reached out a hand toward Lisa. "Why don't we get back to the others?"

The other woman looked at it, hesitated, but took it and just as she did Sabrina was sure she'd made a mistake, that Lisa would grow fangs and sink them into her outstretched arm. Instead her hand was gripped with a frantic strength and Lisa allowed herself to be pulled to a standing position.

"Come on. It's okay."

A glance at the back door—the reason she'd come back here in the first place--confirmed was locked then Sabrina backed a step toward the doorway. Once again she was nervous, some inner part of her warning her to just go. Instead, she pulled Lisa along, gently, but choosing not to turn her back to the woman. Something about Lisa's complete silence unnerved Sabrina. True, Lisa had always been more reserved, but this one was practically catatonic.

"Come on," Sabrina repeated.

She half stumbled through the doorway, tripping over the carpet, and made the decision to turn her back. As she led Lisa down the hallway it felt wrong, dangerous, and Sabrina glanced back. Lisa's dead-eyed stare unnerved her. The eyes rolled around to focus on Sabrina with a glaring look of malevolence toward her. It lasted a second then was gone.

Had she imagined it?

Lisa continued to move forward at the same speed as Sabrina. She made no move to attack. They moved foot by foot toward the front office until the murmur of voices drifted toward them.

Lisa gave a grunt. Her eyes widened.

"It's okay," she repeated, not knowing what else to say.

Sabrina finally passed through the doorway and into the entry once again. Everyone stood in much the same positions they had when she'd left.

"Look who I found," she said.

Sabrina backed into the room a step, allowing room for Lisa to follow. The other woman stopped in the doorway, one hand rubbing at the opposite arm. Eyes darting and full of suspicion.

"Lisa!" Abby said, relief breaking through her panic momentarily.

Nick shook his head. "I thought you said the cabin had been torn apart Pat."

Patrick nodded. "There was a lot of blood."

Lisa's eyes darted back and forth, her stance shifted, as if ready to run.

"Careful Sabrina," Nick said. "We saw someone who looked like Ben tonight, only it wasn't him."

Lisa's lips drew back, revealing teeth red with blood.

"Ben!" she said, but it came out garbled, like she had a mouthful of something. Her eyes widened and she screamed it. "Ben!!!!!"

The others recoiled.

Erik jumped to his feet. "That's *not* Lisa."

TWENTY-NINE

Lisa tried to retreat, teeth pulled back in a grimace that wasn't the gentle woman they all knew. Her hands came up, fingers hooked and ready to scratch someone's eyes out.

"Ben!!!!" Lisa, or the thing that looked like Lisa, wailed

Nick and Pat were on their feet as well, Abby shrunk back to one side.

"Grab her!" Nick warned.

Sabrina stood stunned a moment but quickly recovered. She took hold of one arm while the guys rushed over to help. Blood drooled down Lisa's chin. She fought like a wild animal as they forced her into a chair.

"Find something to tie her with," Nick said.

Nick and Erik held the thing which looked like Lisa in the chair while the others searched. Abby found several extension cords in one drawer and brought them over.

"Ben!!!" The Lisa-thing wailed again, spraying blood from her mouth.

They took the longer extensions and secured the woman's torso. Shorter ones were used to hold her arms. The fight immediately went out of her and she sagged into the chair, eyes on the floor.

"Where is the real Lisa?" Nick asked.

No response, just more glaring.

"Why were you in the back room?" Erik demanded.

Nothing.

"Hold on guys," Patrick said, getting down to look into her face. "Lisa, if it is you, you have to talk to us."

A quick shake of her head.

Won't talk? Or not Lisa?

"What did you mean you'd seen someone who looked like Ben?" Sabrina asked.

"Just that. He looked like Ben. He sounded like Ben. But he punched a hole in Rob and..." Nick's voice broke. "And pulled out his heart."

"Jesus," Sabrina breathed.

She stared at Lisa, trying to reconcile the almost catatonic woman she'd found against the thing which had killed Rob. It felt different, but that didn't mean it wasn't dangerous to all of them.

"There was blood all over that cabin," Patrick repeated. "You saw it, Nick."

"I saw it."

Patrick shook his head, unsure if he was justifying his actions of tying Lisa to the chair, or convincing the others that there was something wrong with the picture.

Something felt off though.

Why had all the fight gone out of Lisa?

"Guys?" Pat started.

"I know Pat." Nick placed one hand on his friend's shoulder. "But we can't take a chance on her."

Nick was right of course.

Was this really only something that looked like Lisa? Like the thing Nick encountered which looked like Ben. Pat wanted to let her go, to speak sense to them, but found Nick's caution made more sense. He could point out that Nick, Erik and he himself had been alone before coming together again, that any of them could have been similarly taken over. Would that just create more paranoia? They needed to work together.

Each of *them* was acting normal.

Patrick looked to Nick and saw a resignation in his face. They'd been right, they couldn't take the chance. Erik let out a sigh and turned his back on the woman in the chair. Sabrina shook her head and also looked away. Abby continued to scrutinize her.

"Okay," Sabrina said. "So, what next?"

Everyone looked to Patrick who felt the weight of their expectations, wondering why he was suddenly leader. He'd never been the driving force in their group. That was more Gillian and Miles. Rob occasionally.

None of whom were there.

Leader by default.

"Next?" Patrick said. "We do what we set out to do. We barricade ourselves in here for the night. Doors are secure. Let's make sure the windows are locked too."

"And look for weapons?" Erik suggested.

"Sure," Pat agreed, though he wondered what weapon would do anything against the things they'd seen so far. Wendigo. Axe-man. Crazy cook. Doppelganger. "Yes, then we come back here and talk about Theo's stories."

"What do you mean?" Nick asked.

"We should try to remember any other characters that might come knocking on the door."

THIRTY

Securing the rest of the office took little time. There was no way to make the building anything near impregnable. Best they could do was ensure that if someone, some*thing... any*thing came that they were aware. The desk blocking the front door was as good as that was going to get. They moved a heavy metal file cabinet from the copy room in front of the back door. Even so, the place had enough windows that would be obvious entrances in the most basic horror movie. Best they could do with those was make sure the locks were in place and hope these monsters didn't deal in such tropes.

All their efforts were the equivalent of whistling past the graveyard. It gave them some small feeling of control though any of those monsters would make quick work of their barriers. The axe-man alone would get through that front door with relative ease.

And the doppelganger could already be among them.

Lisa sagged against her restraints, staring at the floor.

Planning an escape? Or just an exhausted victim?

Patrick wandered toward the back office, mind churning.

Lisa was the most suspicious but Nick and Erik were the only survivors of their groups. Were either who they seemed? He himself had been alone for some time after Gillian disappeared. Why should he be above suspicion? What about Abby? Sabrina had left her behind and either one could have been taken.

Was the doppelganger already among them?

"Stop it!" he hissed.

"What?"

Patrick had been passing Gillian's office and found Erik behind the desk, rifling through the drawers.

"What's your problem?" Erik demanded.

Pat waved it off. "Just my thoughts getting away from me."

Erik rolled his eyes and continued his search.

"What are you looking for?"

"Bullets."

"Bullets? What for?"

Erik held up a handgun.

"That was in Gillian's desk?"

"Yep." Erik opened the next drawer.

He didn't close the previous one, just let it hang open. It irked Pat but he wasn't sure if it was because of his borderline OCD, or the lack of respect for Gillian.

"Why wouldn't she get that when we were all here earlier?" Patrick asked.

"No idea. Maybe she didn't think anything was wrong enough yet?"

"Maybe." Patrick considered the gun and the situation. Last time they'd been in this office the trees had closed in and the phone was dead. Surely that would have been enough to convince Gillian there was danger. Unless—

"Unless there *are* no bullets."

Erik looked up. "Why would she have a gun and no bullets?"

"For show. For the threat."

Erik sighed and sank back into the office chair. It made a certain kind of sense. This was a kid's camp and having a loaded gun around was asking for trouble. Then again, this was a kid's camp and if some parent showed up who shouldn't have access to their kid...

"Maybe," Erik admitted. "There's certainly no bullets that I can find. Still..."

He slipped the handgun into his jacket pocket.

"What good will that do?" Patrick asked.

"For show," Erik repeated the words back. "For the threat."

Sabrina appeared at the door behind them. "Look what I found."

Held up with both hands was a dull grey sledge hammer, maybe four feet long, with a handle that still held flecks of its original red colour.

"Can you swing that?" Erik asked.

"Try me."

"Given the right circumstances, hmm?"

Sabrina gave a nod and continued toward the front office.

"Two weapons," Erik said. "One with no ammunition and the other too heavy for the carrier to swing."

"You want to take it away from her?"

"Not yet," Erik admitted.

Patrick turned to follow Sabrina and his gaze landed on the old property map on the wall. Again, he was struck by how large the area was. It stretched further to the east than expected, past the maintenance man's house and down the boating road and beyond.

"Something important?" Erik asked, coming up behind him.

"Hmm? Oh, not really. Just bigger than I thought."

The two headed back to the front office where they joined the others, sitting around the smallish room. Lisa was in one chair while Abby took the other. Erik disappeared for a moment then returned with the one from Gillian's office. He offered it to Sabrina.

"That hammer is heavy," he said. "Conserve your strength."

He took the corner of one desk as his own seat. Nick looked around and shrugged, sitting on the floor with his back against a wall. Pat elected to stand.

"One of us should be on watch until morning," Pat said.

"Hour and a half each?" Nick suggested.

"Close enough. Anyone want to go first?"

Sabrina and Erik both raised a hand but he gestured toward her in a *ladies first* gesture.

"I'll go second then."

Nick chose the following shift then Pat, ending with Abby.

"You really think we'll get out in the morning?" Erik asked.

Pat shrugged. "I'm hoping."

"The cold insanity of the situation will be burned away by the morning's sun?"

"Something like that."

Lisa laughed then, looking up. The blood had dried against her chin but more spat out now as she glanced around at them. She laughed again, then resumed staring at nothing in particular, like someone in shock who'd gone through some sort of hell.

"Creepy fucking bitch," Sabrina said and looked away.

"Anyone remember Theo's other stories?" Nick asked.

"The Fluffies," Abby said. "Cute little balls of fluff rolling through the forest."

"Um," Nick offered. "There was also King Raccoon and Lady Tadpole."

Patrick nodded. "All the positive ones. I don't think we need to worry about them. Any other scary ones?"

"Leviticus," Erik muttered.

"What?"

"The monster that lived at the bottom of the lake."

"Oh, yeah. Forgot about that one."

"Angry gnome?" Sabrina offered. Then continued on after getting blank stares. "The gnome would join a cabin and pretend to be one of the kids. He was pissed because the kids got attention while he got rocks thrown at him."

"Huh."

"The laundry monster," Pat said. "It was Theo's attempt to make the laundry room creepier."

"Like that was needed," Abby said.

"The crying boy," Nick added. "The living tree."

"Counsellor Tommy's ghost."

"Black dog."

"The mole people."

Eventually they ran down.

"Jesus," Erik said. "Any one of these things is enough. Never mind his entire portfolio of shit."

"There's probably more," Nick said with a yawn, "but I'm beat."

It wasn't ridiculously late but the day had drained them all and there was an entire night to get through. They decided to retire except for Sabrina who stood, sledge hammer in hand, guarding them in their sleep.

Interlude 7 – 20 Years Ago – King Racoon, Lady Tadpole, and friends

THEO RAN one hand down his face. It was a hot day with little cloud cover, but that wasn't what had him sweating.

"You okay?"

"Hmm?" He turned toward the sound of the voice.

Abby smiled up at him and he nodded.

"You'll be great," she said. "It's just another story."

"Hah! Yeah."

It *was* just another story, but not what he was used to telling. First of all, it was to the entire camp, during the daytime, on the upper compound. Worse, it wasn't a creepy story, this was the positive characters of camp. Pre-existing ones who were created by previous staff, not his own.

"Not like you have a choice," Abby added.

"Well, when you put it like that."

He'd gotten shit after telling the axe-man story. Not so much for the story itself, but for causing such a commotion and waking several of the younger cabins. Anytime there was screaming after dark it set everyone on edge, especially the camp director.

This was his penance.

"You're right, Abby. Thanks for the reminder."

"I didn't mean—"

"Nope, all good. I truly mean it. Thank you. Puts it in perspective."

"Okay. Well, they're all waiting for you."

"Show time."

He walked to the center of the amassed staff and

campers. They were arranged around him in a circle, theatre in the round style. That was good. He would have to keep moving, no time to look at any one person too long. He raised one hand, the signal to call for quiet. Slowly everyone else did the same until silence reigned.

"I hope you all enjoy these stories. They're not my usual thing but... well, here we go."

He gathered his thoughts and got focussed. He knew where to start anyway.

"King Raccoon and Lady Tadpole watched over this mountain long before Camp White Bear came along. They found they loved the children so much, though they don't have any of their own, and made sure to watch over camp and everyone here. They love the sound of laughter and joy. The sounds of the daytime."

He had to sneak that in there.

"They have other friends who live in the forest too. Ones who keep watch when you are in the woods during the day. The Fluffies live all around, occupying the trees and bushes. If you look hard enough you may just find one while on a nature walk. They make sure no one gets lost."

His eyes caught Mary-Louise and Sarah, picked them out from the crowd. They sat, staring at him, neither openly scoffing. They looked like older siblings needing to attend something for a little brother or sister.

"Then there are the triplets. Ike, Spike, and Bartholomew. They watch the roads and make sure any holes get filled in. During the day they build things, like all of the cabins and other buildings, and at night they watch over the dreams of campers. When you have a nice dream, it is because of them."

This was his own addition. He needed some sort of fantastic element to it all.

"So, if you're having a nightmare, make sure you call out to one of those three. They will come and chase any bad dreams away."

That was an attempt to mitigate any 'damage' done by his scary stories—the camp director's words, not his. For the rest of the summer he would get to tell these sugar-bomb stories to the entire camp. Every Sunday before picnics.

But at night he vowed to keep telling the good stuff. He just needed to be careful about it.

CHAPTER

THIRTY-ONE

Awareness came back to Patrick slowly, the way it did after a full night's sleep.

He sat bolt upright and looked around. No daylight streamed in through the window so it must still be middle of the night... but it felt later. He grabbed for the useless phone which sat on the floor next to him.

"Seven-thirty?"

Impossible.

But it wasn't. Pat felt the time was correct. Nick hadn't woken him last night for his shift, and lay close by, snoring.

"Nick! Wake up."

"Huh!" Nick shifted, then suddenly remembering everything sat up and looked around. "What? What's wrong?"

"You didn't wake me for watch last night."

Nick looked toward the window. "It's still night."

"It's after seven."

"What?"

"Check your phone."

Nick did and shook his head, feeling the trueness of the time as well. "No one woke me."

"Me either," Erik said from across the office.

Abby was sitting up as well, eyes wild and staring all around. "Where's Sabrina?"

Everyone was suddenly in a flurry of activity. Erik went to the back office and was only gone a moment when he called for everyone. They found him standing in front of the wide-open back door. The file cabinet had been shoved aside.

"Did Sabrina do this?" Nick asked.

Abby shrugged. "Why would she?"

Erik turned to Patrick. "Still think this will all be over with sunup?"

"No," Patrick admitted. "Let's get that cabinet back in place."

Nick muscled it back in front of the now closed door then they turned and headed back to the front office.

"Hey!" Erik said, crossing to the desk blocking the front door. Lying across it was the sledge hammer Sabrina had claimed. Erik hefted it in one hand. "She wouldn't have just left this."

Nick shrugged. "Maybe it got too heavy?"

"Did you see the way she held that thing last night?"

"It had to have happened in the first hour and a half," Patrick said. "Before she was supposed to wake Erik."

"I didn't hear anything," Erik said.

Patrick glanced at Lisa, still tied to the chair, trying to reposition. Eyes blinking.

"Did you see anything?" Patrick asked her.

A shake of her head. She looked around, as if wondering how she'd gotten there.

"Hep me."

Patrick crouched down in front of her. Lisa spoke like she had cotton stuffed in her mouth.

"Patick. Pease hep me."

"Lisa. I—"

She opened her mouth then, tears rolling down her face.

Blood caked her chin and teeth, but inside...

"Oh, god."

She was missing her tongue.

"Jesus! What happened Lisa?"

Nick and Erik came up behind him to stare at the woman in the chair.

"Careful Pat," Nick warned. "Remember how tricky the doppelgangers are."

Abby inched closer to Nick, as if his proximity would keep her safe.

"I eed to ee," Lisa said.

"Pee?" Erik said. "Forget it."

Lisa sobbed. "Pease."

"I'll take her," Abby said.

"Pease," she repeated.

"We can't take a chance," Erik said.

Patrick was already untying her. "We can't just let her piss herself either."

Erik and Nick looked at each other as if this was maybe exactly the plan.

"The doppelganger's power is in people not knowing

they've replaced someone," Patrick explained. "With us suspecting her, if she is a fake, then she has lost that power."

Erik stepped back and held the hammer in a position that suggested he would be ready to swing. Free from the bindings Lisa got to her feet, rubbing at the spots where she'd been bound.

"Come on," Abby said.

Lisa took a step, stumbled, then grabbed Abby by her jacket. She swung the smaller girl around and let go so that she flew toward Erik. He pulled up the hammer in time that Abby didn't get hurt but the two of them collided, driving Erik back against the wall.

By the time any of them moved Lisa was gone, down the hallway into the back office.

Erik pushed Abby aside and rushed after Lisa, the others on his heels. They rounded the corner to see the bathroom door slamming closed. The click of the lock sounded off the hallway walls. Erik looked at the hammer in his hands then at the door.

"Come out of there," Nick demanded, banging on the door.

No response. Sobbing from inside.

The old plywood doors wouldn't stand up to more than one or two strikes from that hammer. Erik lifted it, ready to start by smashing the knob.

"No, wait!" Abby said.

The others turned, as if forgetting she'd even been in the room.

"Why not just lock her in?"

Erik, Nick, and Patrick looked to each other then back to Abby.

"How?" Nick asked.

Abby gestured at the doorknob of the bathroom, then at the one for the file room next door. Close together. "Use the extension cord. Tie one knob to the other."

Erik laughed. "Simple yet brilliant."

He rushed back to the entry and returned with one of the long extension cords that had secured Lisa all night, starting to loop one end around the knob.

"Are we so sure this isn't really Lisa?" Patrick asked.

Erik stopped. "We all agreed last night."

"She's missing her tongue, for god's sake," Patrick said.

Erik lowered the hammer, placing the head against the floor. The four looked around at each other, waiting for some extra thoughts.

"But..." Abby said.

Everyone looked at her, wondering if she would follow up the idea of tying the door closed with another intelligent observation.

"Well... who took Sabrina?"

The guys all looked at each other then back again.

"Someone had to move that cabinet," she said. "If Lisa didn't take Sabrina, who did?"

"Lisa was tied all night too," Patrick reminded.

"But would that stop her, if she's a doppelganger?"

They all turned toward the locked bathroom door and took a step back. If this Lisa was something like that and able to free herself in the night, then would that makeshift lock hold her?

"If that *is* Lisa," Nick said, turning toward Patrick, "then she's safer in there than we are out here."

Patrick stared at the door a moment longer. "Probably."

"We need food, man," Erik said.

It was the first mention of it, and now that the idea had been let loose everyone felt it. Their dinner last night had been unfinished.

Nick nodded. "Let's take care of getting food then come back and talk."

Another glance at the door and Pat nodded. The four grouped together, backing away from the bathroom and heading for the front door.

"Hold on," Erik said and gripped the hammer in a ready to use position. "Okay, ready."

"That didn't help Sabrina," Abby said.

"Still feels better than empty hands."

"You still have that gun," Patrick asked.

"Gun?" Nick said.

Erik gave Patrick a withering look then lowered the hammer so its head rested against the floor. He pulled the handgun from his pocket, handing it toward Nick. "Empty hands or empty handgun."

"An empty gun?" Nick took the weapon anyway. "Figures."

"I was thinking it might scare someone if we pointed it at them."

Nick shrugged. It was slightly better than nothing. He tilted it left and right, holding it like he'd never seen one before.

"You don't know much about guns," Abby said, pressing up against him. "Do you?"

"Does it show?"

She took it from his unresisting hand and tilted it left and right. "Older handgun. A Beretta, I think."

"Umm..." Nick said. "Sure."

She ejected the magazine and retracted the slide. "You're right. Empty."

The three men looked at each other then back at her.

Abby saw the attention on her. "Terry has a gun, for home protection. I took a class to know how to use it, then read a bunch about them."

"Huh!" Nick said and shrugged. "Keep it, Abby. At least you know how to make it look threatening."

She nodded, hiding a smile as she slid it into one pocket, clinking against the bullet she'd taken from Gillian's desk.

The sun still had not made an appearance and at eight o'clock it still looked like two in the morning. Shadows pressed in from all directions. Three flashlights left. Patrick's, Nick's, and Abby's. Erik held the sledge hammer with both hands. They moved as a group down the slight hill, toward the dining hall. Each did their best to look in all directions as they went, keeping their flashlights moving, sure that an attack could happen at any moment.

Nothing happened.

The dining hall never felt like such a long journey. It was few hundred feet from the office but each step they took felt like they were further away. No lights were on in the hall, nothing to tell them that they neared the building.

"Didn't we leave the lights on?" Erik asked.

Shrugs. No one remembered.

They continued to stagger through the dark, counting steps and sure that they should have reached the dining hall long ago.

"Another loop?" Erik said.

They looked back but couldn't see the office now either.

"Forward or back?" Nick asked.

"Forward," Patrick said.

A giggle from the darkness.

Behind them

No one moved.

"The crazy cook," Patrick said.

"What do we do?" Abby wailed.

"Who's the slowpoke?"

THIRTY-TWO

They spun around to see who was last in line. Everyone was still there.

"Make a circle," Patrick said.

Erik shook his head. "What?"

"No one is last if there's no line."

Everyone looked to each other. Nick moved to be next to Patrick. It was half-assed effort at best until Patrick directed each person into place.

"Move forward now," he said.

They moved, hesitantly at first, then with some speed.

A giggle off to their left, but nothing approached.

"This is ridiculous," Erik said, at the opposite side of the circle, facing away and walking backwards.

"You'd rather be last in line?" Nick asked.

No answer.

"Slooooowwwwwpoke," the voice taunted from the dark.

Step by step they continued until the dining hall crept

from the darkness. Thirty feet or so ahead of them, door closed.

"Sinister," Nick said.

Abby nodded.

"We gotta eat," Erik answered. "And if that crazy cook is out here then she isn't inside."

It was logical. It made sense.

Then a shape separated from the shadows and cut past the entry to that building. The four of them froze, lights pointed. The shape moved from view, around a corner.

"What was that?" Abby demanded.

"What was what?" Erik said, trying to turn and see. "What?"

"Don't break the circle," Patrick warned.

Erik grumbled but continued to face back the way they'd come, aware that if he turned he would be last in the group. They started forward again, attention on where that shadow had gone. A few feet from the dining hall's front doors the shape came rushing back, heading for them.

"No!" Patrick yelled.

Erik spun and raised the hammer.

"Wait!" Abby said. "Sabrina?"

The other woman staggered toward them and Nick caught her in his arms.

"The shadows," she muttered. "The shadows."

"Shadows?" Erik said. He turned a circle, looking the opposite direction of everyone else, vary aware that he was the slowpoke at the back of the group now.

"Let's get her inside," Nick said.

Erik huffed out a breath of annoyance as they reached

their destination and jerked open the door. The five rushed into the dining hall, then came to a stop. The room was dark.

Patrick and Abby aimed their lights inside, showing the table with the remains of their dinner. Vague shapes crouched around it, unmoving.

"Hold on," Erik said and slapped his hand against the wall next to the door, searching.

Overhead lights flared into life, painting the room with brightness and revealing what was arranged around the table.

The chairs were occupied by the bodies of their dead friends.

Five remained empty. One for each of them. Only...

"Lisa's spot is empty," Abby observed.

"Wait—" Nick started.

Suddenly he was slammed into from the side, thrown into Patrick. The two of them sprawled to the floor. Above them Sabrina hissed, fingers lengthened to claws. Nick held out one hand in a gesture to ward her off. Erik recovered first, running up behind her, bringing the sledge hammer down between her shoulder blades.

The creature which looked like Sabrina screeched and tumbled forward. Erik raised the hammer over his head again but the monster didn't wait. It rushed forward, leapt onto the nearest table then crashed through window, spraying glass and wood, hurtling out into the night.

"Jesus," Nick muttered, running the hands which had caught Sabrina minutes earlier against the legs of his jeans, as if something nasty coated them. "Fuck, fuck, fuck."

"They're playing with us," Erik said.

The four recovered, standing together and staring out through the shattered window. With a shuddering sigh Abby turned back to their dinner table, the others following. Gillian lay forward in her meal, arms splayed to either side, her face mercifully hidden. Beside her was Sabrina, the real one, leaning back with unseeing eyes focussed on the ceiling.

"We should have noticed her right away," Erik said.

Patrick shrugged, as if to say *give me a break.*

Ben sat up in his seat, face missing with muscle beneath visible. Miles and Rob leaned against each other, with Rob wearing a wide-eyed look of shock, a hole gaping in his abdomen. Jackie sat slumped, skin torn and slashed, bite marks and missing flesh, as if a wild animal had attacked her. Theo lay forward in his unfinished meal as well, severed arm on the table before him.

Abby made a choked, gurgling noise. She stepped back, coming up against the closed door.

"Don't do it, Abby," Patrick said.

She shook her head, gaze coming around to stare at him.

"You back out that door and something *will* get you."

A barely controlled sob and a glance behind her. "Lisa," she said.

"What?"

"Lisa isn't there."

"We already covered that," Erik said.

"That's the real her," Abby said. "Locked in the bathroom."

Patrick nodded.

"We have to get back to her," Abby said.

"We still need food."

"I'm not hungry anymore. Are you?"

Nick shook his head and stepped toward the swinging doors which led to the kitchen. "Right now? No, but I will be."

"But—" Abby began.

The others followed him into the kitchen.

"Quickly," Patrick warned. "Grab what we can and let's go."

"Why?' Erik said. "Why go back?"

"To free Lisa," Patrick said.

Erik huffed out a breath and rolled his eyes. "All the food is here. Someone go get her and bring her back."

"Someone?" Pat asked. "All by themselves?"

"I'm not going back out there."

"I'm not staying here," Abby wailed. "Not with... with..."

She gestured back toward the dining area and their dead friends.

Nick and Abby had gathered the food which would be most easily eaten. Loaves of bread, cheese, deli meat. Nick had an entire flat of bottled water.

"There's more in the fridge," he said, gesturing with his head.

Erik sighed and went to grab some more food.

"I can't pass back through there," Abby said.

"We'll go the back way," Nick said. "Through the kitchen staff's rooms."

Everyone carrying what they could the four headed without hesitation to the door. No one looked back at the grim spectacle behind them. Abby and Patrick carried bags of food draped on their wrists while Nick carried a flat of water under one arm. Each of them had free hands to point flashlights. Erik, by unspoken agreement, kept his hands free to swing the hammer, the picture of him defending the group from the Sabrina lookalike fresh in their minds.

Beyond the door at the end of the kitchen was a short hallway with two rooms on either side and a door on the end leading back toward the upper compound. They rushed through quickly and out into the night once again.

"Should be morning," Erik grumbled.

Patrick nodded agreement. The four kept a tight group, making sure to be on guard for the crazy cook, listening for her giggle. Erik took the lead this time to deal with any approaching threat, and ready to spin back and defend the rear as well. This time Patrick walked backwards to maintain a circle.

No sound of giggles came.

No one called vague threats from the darkness.

They each took steps forward at the same time, like some bizarre synchronized dance.

"Pat," Nick warned.

"What is it?"

"The shadows are moving."

THIRTY-THREE

S hadows.

Unnatural night continued on creating shadows everywhere. The ones Nick warned against moved separately from the surrounding darkness. As sinister as the night around them.

Come closer.

A voice, different from the high mocking one of the cook. Spoken so close.

Pat spun and pointed his light at one particular patch of shadow which dissipated with the illumination. Problem was only three still had working flashlights and there were so many more directions than that.

Abby pointed hers at the same spot Pat did.

"No," he said. "Keep it moving."

Come here, one shadow whispered.

Patrick spun in a circle, trying to shine everywhere at once. When he came back around again the shadows were always closer than before the light had momentarily banished them.

"Move!" Erik said. "Run! Back to the office."

Erik dropped the sledge hammer from his ready stance and held it across his body to run instead. What good was a hammer against a shadow? Might as well punch the air.

He nudged Abby ahead of him, not so hard she would lose balance but gently and persistently to keep her moving through the panic. Her light cut a path through the dark ahead. Nick followed behind Erik, carrying his load of water, while Pat took the back, shining his light left, right, back. Over and over.

Join us.

The office was within reach. They could see it.

Light still shone from inside.

Left. Right. Back.

Abby's light pushed a path toward the office.

Come closer.

Abby screamed and dropped her flashlight.

One of the shadows had reached out from the side and touched her arm. It burned like fire where the touch had landed. Pat pointed his light at her and forced the shadow back again, taking a touch to the back himself while Erik scooped up Abby's flashlight and led the way.

"Come on!"

Come here!

A shadowed hand landed on Erik's left shoulder, dragging a scream from his throat, but he managed to keep grip on both the flashlight and hammer. Pat tried to shine everywhere at once. Nick let out a yell of pain and fear and shock.

Pat returned the light to him.

"Fuck that hurts!" Nick said.

The shirt on Nick's right had been burned away and the flesh beneath was darker. Pat felt another hand on his back, right in the center, lingering. He spun but the shadow and pain spun with him. It felt like something burrowing between his shoulder blades. The arm on that side went numb and he had just enough presence of mind to switch hands for the flashlight, though the loaves of bread he carried were lost. He brought the light up over his shoulder and shone it behind him. The pain eased, but the numbness remained.

Come here!

Come closer!

Erik and Abby reached the steps of the office, not hesitating but rushing right inside. Pat and Nick were only steps behind. Nick yelled out again and stumbled as the shadows went for his legs, one burning spot on each.

Join us! The shadows hissed.

Pain washed through Pat fresh at a spot on his side.

"Fuck off!" he yelled.

From the doorway Erik pointed the light back toward them, making a path to the office and allowing Pat to focus his elsewhere. He grabbed Nick under one arm, helping him back to his feet and up the steps. Nick half ran, half crawled through the door and skidded across the wood floor on the opposite side. His flat of water slamming down and sliding further. Pat backed through, his flashlight combined with Erik's forcing the shadows back. Erik slammed the door.

Nick lifted his shirt, trying to see behind him, onto his own back. Abby came over.

"It looks like this."

Nick looked at a spot on her upper arm, a vaguely hand shaped mark. It had turned black, as if burned with a torch. In fact, it had the appearance of a shadow itself. Everyone had more than one spot on them like this. Arms. Back. Side. Erik had one on his neck. The marks all continued to burn like fire.

"Ben was right," Erik said.

The others looked at him, questioning.

"When he said the shadows story scared him most," Erik explained.

Had that really been less than twenty-four hours ago?

Nick ripped into the water bottles and tore the cap off one. He flipped it over and allowed the liquid to run down his back, sighing as the burning eased, fading away. The patch of darkness on his skin remained.

"That's better," he sighed. "Try it."

Everyone grabbed their own bottle and followed Nick's example, sighing with the relief it brought. They waited for the pain and burning to return but it seemed the water was enough to banish it.

"Lisa!" Abby said.

Pat cursed, remembering their missing friend from around the table. Abby led the rush to the locked bathroom, the others following. Erik flipped every light switch as he passed. At the bathroom the electrical cord remained in place around the knobs.

"Lisa!" Pat called. "Hold on. We'll have you out in a second."

No answer.

Erik worked at untying the cord and freeing the knob. It took seconds which seemed like hours. Then the door was thrown inward.

Abby gasped.

Nick groaned.

Pat cursed again.

Inside the small bathroom the window had been hacked into a wide hole. Glass and wood littered the inside bathroom. Blood was everywhere.

This time it was Lisa's for sure.

THIRTY-FOUR

"We're dead," Abby said in a flat tone, staring into the blood-soaked bathroom.

"Abby—" Patrick started,

"Don't you fucking dare," she said rounding on Patrick, one finger pointed up into his face. "Don't tell me we'll be fine. Don't tell me to not panic. Just don't."

Patrick nodded, eyes wide and hands up. "You're right."

Abby stopped, face relaxing, finger dropping to her side. She'd been hoping one of them had some sort of plan. "So what do we do?"

Erik gestured at the food sprawled across the office floor. "Breakfast?"

She turned to stare at a loaf of bread that had rolled up against the wall. "Breakfast?"

"Why not?"

Abby shrugged. She started to sit in the chair Lisa had

occupied all night then thought better of it. She crossed to the other one and sat.

"Take the chair, Nick," Patrick said.

Nick limped to it without protest. He hadn't poured water on his leg wounds yet and found the burning increased if ignored. He'd been planning to water them when Abby started the rush for poor Lisa. Now he sat and opened one bottle while Pat and Erik brought the groceries to the desk and spread them out. Bread. Jam. Pastries. Croissants. Cheese. Lunch meat.

"Well, if we're still alive at lunch," Erik said, grabbing a pastry. "We can have another final meal."

"Erik," Patrick started.

"No!" Abby spat out, slapping one hand against the desk. "I did not kiss my children goodbye when I left."

The three men looked one to another with shrugs but no ability to look into each other's eyes.

"What do you suggest?" Nick asked.

"Not like we can go anywhere," Erik observed. "Those shadows are deadly and until the sun rises, they're all over the place."

"So we just sit here and wait for them to come get us?" Abby asked. "That hole in the bathroom wall tells me we aren't safe in here."

"I—" Patrick started. "I... No. There must be something we can do."

"Can we just eat first?" Erik said. "One normal thing."

Abby nodded. "I can agree to that."

Nick and Patrick joined them and settled in to eat a breakfast. Maybe their last. They grabbed anything they wanted, having more than the four of them would need for the next day.

"So... Um..." Abby said around a mouthful of lemon pastry. "What have you guys been doing for the last twenty years?"

Everyone looked to each other, waiting for someone else to go first. Nick finally shrugged and wiped the sticky jam on his fingers against his pants, leaving a purple smear against blue jeans.

"I'll go first," he said. "I went to university, got a teaching degree and have a position teaching phys. ed. at a school in a low-income area."

"Kids from The Bear," Erik observed.

"A few."

"So no change in your life."

Nick laughed. "Hey, I like teaching kids, and I'm good at it."

"None of your own?" Abby asked.

"Nope. I was married briefly and am now happily divorced."

A couple of laughs from that. Abby just had a thoughtful look. When it was obvious no other details were coming Erik swallowed. No change in expression or demeanor.

"I spent four years in prison," he said, "for dealing drugs and other shitty stuff."

"Oh, Erik," Abby said.

"Hey, no judgements, okay? I have regrets but they made me who I am today. It is what it is."

He took another bit of croissant and shrugged.

"No judgements," Abby said with a nod. "Okay. Well, I

married a guy with a good job that I don't love in the least. He gave me the kids he wanted and I got a house and lifestyle I wanted."

No response from anyone.

"I love my kids, she continued, "but I wish I'd taken the time to travel, and go to university, and lots of other stuff. I..." She gestured with one hand holding a second pastry. Tears brimmed the edges of her eyes. "No judgements, lots of regrets."

Pat placed one hand on top of hers and she nodded her thanks, not trusting herself to speak.

"I work a boring job" Patrick jumped in, giving Abby a break. "It pays well, but I couldn't care less about it all. "I was never happier than when I worked here and I've never found anything to compare to it."

"So, now that you're back," Nick said, "how does it match up against your memories?"

Patrick stared at his old friend for a moment before breaking into a laugh. Nick joined him and a moment later so did Abby and Erik. They laughed a bit harder than the joke deserved but it broke some tension.

None of them mentioned that the words spoken by each of them had a feeling of last confessions.

Abby sighed. "So, that's it then?"

"I don't see a solution," Nick said. "Doesn't mean there isn't one."

Erik shrugged. "We tried to get out several ways and even got attacked going to the dining hall and back. What option is left?"

"I wish Theo was here," Patrick said.

"I wish he was here instead of me," Erik quipped.

"Really?"

Erik's mouth dropped into an O as he thought of Theo's body in the dining hall. He shook his head against the memory. "Didn't think that comment out."

"What could Theo do?" Abby asked. "He told the stories, he didn't command them."

"What do you mean?"

Abby gave a waving gesture, toward the cabins. "Back then Theo always felt like the stories told themselves. Most of them just came to him."

"Huh!"

"I still think he might have more insight than any of us."

"Maybe. Maybe." A moment's silence and Abby took another breath and forged on. "What about the positive stories?"

"What? King Raccoon?" Erik asked. "Princess Toadstool?"

"Lady Tadpole."

"Yeah, her. What about them?"

"Well, where are they in all of this?"

"Theo told those stories during the daytime," Patrick said. "We may need sunlight for those to show up."

"Sunlight," Erik answered. "Good luck on that."

Nick grunted an acknowledgment, croissant halfway to his mouth when a noise from the back office stopped them all.

Final Interlude – 20 Years Ago – Lord Nightmare

Tonight he had his best audience. There was Mary-Louise, and Sarah. Jaspal was there. Heath. The twins Gary and Randy. All the ones who enjoyed his stories on some level or another. This would be his final story of the summer, and it was one that had been rolling around inside his head for a while.

It was ready to be told.

"You all know King Raccoon, Lady Tadpole, and all the others?"

A couple of groans, an eyeroll from Jaspal.

"I know, I know. Those are a bit too sweet for your tastes."

Mary-Louise laughed.

They'd all been hearing those stories during his mandated story time at picnics and stuff.

"What you don't realize is that they are necessary to balance out the bad, the truly evil."

"Like the axe-man," Sarah offered.

"Or Leviticus." Jaspal.

Heath. "The Shadows."

"Yes, all of those," Theo agreed. "But, just like King Racoon is in charge of all the good ones, the bad ones have a leader too."

"Who?" Randy asked

"What?" his brother said at the same time.

"Lord Nightmare."

A couple of shudders at the name. Perfect.

"The king of the graveyard. It's the center of all his

power. A monster who wants to take over everything, all the fun and light. He wants to steal the laughter and the smiles."

"You've never told us about him," Mary-Louise said.

"No, I guess I haven't, and do you know why?"

Shakes of the head all around.

"Because Lord Nightmare scares even me."

"No," Sarah whispered.

"Mostly Lord Nightmare waits in the background and directs the other monsters. He will point them in a certain direction or give a suggestion. But now..."

Theo paused, unsure of where to go with this. He liked the idea of an overarching villain who was in charge of all things bad. Ideas came to him which seemed true to the character, but now that he had started, he was finding Lord Nightmare a bit too dark to share.

"But now?" Jaspal asked.

Oh well, in for a penny as the old saying goes. "Now, he is coming awake. Do you know where one like Lord Nightmare goes to wreak havoc?"

Wreak havoc? Really?

Tone it down Theo, this is summer camp, not Shakespeare in the park.

A bunch of head shakes.

Heath raised one timid hand. "In nightmares?"

"Exactly. He travels from one camper's nightmare to another, even the staff's, and turns them all from fun to fear. He will steal the light and sunshine and replace it with shadows."

"That's why King Racoon is around," Heath suggested. "And the Fluffies."

Charlie nodded. "And the triplets, Ike, Spike, and Bartholomew."

Theo considered that a moment, mind whirling and trying to assimilate the suggestion. King Racoon had already existed before he came along but he'd made all those positive characters into his own over the tellings on picnic Sundays. They were more than just the saccharine two-dimensional characters he'd started with.

"That's right," he confirmed.

They were real now.

Well, real to him... and to the kids.

He looked at Gillian who leaned near the door, head cocked in a questioning way. Patrick looked a bit confused. Nick and Rob had glanced at each other. Only Abby stared at him with a look that encouraged him to continue.

"Well, I guess what you really want to hear is a scary story though, right?"

"Yeah!" Mary-Louise whispered.

"Well, okay then." Theo cleared his throat and looked around at the assembled campers. "Have you noticed this summer that there have been more nightmares than usual?"

Some nods. Some head shakes.

"If you said no, you're lucky. Most of us have been under attack by Lord Nightmare in our dreams. He visits in the darkest hours when we're too afraid to even go to the bathroom."

The kids had leaned forward, hanging on his words. Gillian now had her arms crossed while Patrick, Nick and Rob were all focussed again.

"The happy dreams are food for him, and when he comes

to take them away, he leaves behind something scary. We all know what happens when we turn the light off."

"Darkness," Jaspal said.

"Yep. And do you know what happens to the dreamers?"

"No," one of the twins said, maybe both of them in unison.

"They start to forget who they are. They forget their homes and their parents. If they forget too much then they just fade away. They disappear into the nightmare world forever. That's what happened to Jaimie."

Everyone knew Jaimie. A well-loved member on staff. It was their first year and they taught arts and crafts, but he needed to leave early.

"He left to go to school," Heath said.

"That's what he told everyone, but he'd already started to forget. He knew he was fading away."

"Poor Jamie," Sarah said.

Gillian scoffed and rolled her eyes. When a couple of kids turned toward her, she turned it into a cough and kept her eyes on Theo.

"But Jamie isn't alone. There are others. People fading into the nightmare world. Counsellors. Kitchen staff. Campers. Do you know how to spot them?"

More head shakes.

"They look tired. Unrested. Struggling each morning to wake up."

Several kids turned to look at Rob and Nick who were notorious among staff for sneaking out of their cabin at night to visit girlfriends.

"What about you?" Theo asked. "Are you more tired than usual in the morning? Are you starting to fade away?"

Some looks of real worry on the kids faces, even on some of his favorites. No, he was right, this character was too dark. Gillian was already showing signs of gathering her kids and leaving. He needed to end this on a positive note.

"So, when you are feeling that way in the morning, you make sure you call out to King Raccoon for help."

THIRTY-FIVE

The four made their way down the hallway, heading cautiously forward. Erik took the front, hammer at the ready.

"Where did that noise come from?" Abby asked. "What was it?"

"How should I know?" Erik snapped. "Could have been papers falling over for all we know."

"So, room to room search," Patrick said.

"Yeah, I guess."

The first door led to the bathroom which still looked like a slaughter. Lisa's blood covered the walls and floor, a gaping hole in the back wall big enough to drag a person through. It was like a punch in the gut.

Nothing moved outside and Patrick closed the door again.

"Next," he sighed.

The storage room. They pushed the door open and stood

looking, waiting for some sign of what had made the noise. Something. Anything.

"Nope," Nick finally decided.

Moving along they came to Gillian's office.

"Didn't we leave this door open?" Erik asked.

They looked face to face. None could recall closing it, or a reason why they would have done so.

"Yeah, that's what I thought." He stood with hammer raised, ready for anything that might come out of the room.

He gave a nod to Nick who twisted the knob and threw it open. Inside the room looked as they remembered. The light was now off which was wrong. They'd rushed around turning all the lights on when they returned.

Nick pushed into the room and flicked the switch, scanning the surroundings. Behind him came Erik who stood near the door. ready to swing at anything that moved.

Patrick circled around the desk and came to a stop.

"What is it?" Nick asked.

Patrick mouthed *under the desk*.

A nod from Erik and he came over to bop the desk's top with his sledge hammer. It was a struggle not to just bring it down through the top and into whatever was underneath.

"Come out," he demanded.

"Can't be a monster," Nick said. "They wouldn't hide."

"Lisa?" Abby rushed around the desk and looked into the gap. She stumbled backward with a cry of disgust.

Erik brought his hammer up again.

"Don't hurt me," a voice croaked.

"Then get your ass out here!"

"Easy Erik," Patrick warned, getting down on one knee.

"Jesus, Pat," Nick warned. "Careful."

"Yeah, you that anxious for a reunion with the others?" Erik said.

Patrick ignored them, hand out. "It's okay. We won't hurt you."

A gnarled hand reached out tentatively. It was spotted green and brown with long nails. Abby had returned to the far side of the desk again, next to Nick. Patrick gently pulled the owner of that hand forward, bringing it into the light. The creature was less than three feet high with a greenish complexion and bulging eyes. The hair was short and looked as if it had been cut with a lawnmower.

"Who are you?" Patrick asked.

"B... Bartholomew."

"One of the triplets?" Nick asked.

From the light side of Theo's stories, though this had the appearance of one of his monsters. Bartholomew looked like he'd been through hell.

"What are you doing here?" Erik demanded.

"I keep moving..." the creature said. "Keep ahead of the monsters."

Erik cut back a response about this thing calling others monsters.

Abby cut in. "Where are your brothers?"

"Ike," Bartholomew said in a low voice. A shake of his head. "Dead. Spike. Dead. Only I escaped to the world between worlds."

"You..." Patrick started and considered his words. A shrug and he forged ahead. "You can die?"

A slow nod. "In the dream land, in the storyland. Yes."

"Who did this?' Abby asked.

"Lord Nightmare."

"Why?"

"Why? Because he's Lord Nightmare," Bartholomew spit out. He scoffed and looked aside. "No. There's more."

"More?"

"A ritual. A prophecy."

The four stayed silent, giving the small creature a chance to think. Finally he took a deep breath and let it loose as a long sigh.

"The prophecy. It tells of gaining infinite power for a finite period."

"Infinite...?" Erik said.

"Yes. With that Lord Nightmare would cross into the real world."

"Cross over?" Patrick asked. "But you crossed over without any ritual."

"No, not really. Your camp is in a place between the worlds right now. I can exist here. So can Luthor, Doris, and the shadows. As long as this land exists."

Patrick looked to the others and shrugged.

"That's not enough for Lord Nightmare though. For years he has tasted the waking world through children's night-mares, and now he's found how to get it for himself."

"A finite period," Erik said. "How finite?"

Ike shrugged. "Mere minutes. Enough to get all he wants."

"Okay, so what's the ritual?" Nick asked, thinking it the obvious question. "How does he fulfill this prophecy?"

Bartholomew shook his head and stepped back then

steeled himself, hands at his side clenched into fists. "The first part was the death of my friends and family. Twelve of us in the story lands. King Raccoon. Lady Tadpole. My brothers, Ike and Spike. The woodsman and the Crying Boy. Fancy Nancy. And four of the Fluffies. I saw what was happening and ran."

Abby counted on her fingers. "That's only eleven."

"He also sacrificed Leviticus."

"Leviticus?" Erik said. "Isn't that one of the monsters?"

"Leviticus was too powerful for Lord Nightmare, too hard to control."

"So he got his twelve," Nick said.

"Yes. This part of the ritual gives him a store of power for the next part."

Nick said. "What's next?"

"Cutting this land off from the living world. This gives one small area to control which is easier than the storylands or the real world."

"But that is his end goal," Patrick said. "The whole world."

"Oh, yes."

"Great!" Erik exploded. "Wonderful! Not bad enough we're being killed, now we have to stop the end of the world."

"Okay, so the first two steps are done," Nick said. "What comes next?"

"A sacrifice of twelve of your side of existence. This creates the bridge for Lord Nightmare and the monsters."

"Twelve?" Patrick said, looking to his friends. "All of us."

"Eight so far," Nick said, counting them off on his fingers. "Ben, Rob, Miles, Lisa, Gillian, Sabrina, Theo, and Jackie."

"Like we don't know who's dead," Erik said.

Abby added. "Doris and Claude too, no? Don't they count?"

The four turned to Bartholomew who considered. "They died on this property? In this world between worlds?"

"Yes."

"Then they would indeed count as sacrifices."

"Ten then," Patrick sighed.

"Hold on," Abby said. "The campsites and the maintenance man's house, those were camp property, but the cottages?"

Nick shook his head. "Miles thought we should have still been on camp property when we got to the cottages. One of them was Ben's. It was all a trick."

"Okay, whatever," Erik said. "What's the next part of the ritual."

"Nothing. That is all Lord Nightmare needs to do."

"Two more," Erik said, glancing at the others as if deciding which two.

"So what do we do?" Patrick asked.

"You need to disrupt the ritual."

"How?"

"The final sacrifice needs to happen at the graveyard."

Erik dropped the hammer to his side. "Well, that should be easy to avoid since the graveyard isn't part of camp."

"Hold on!" Patrick snapped his fingers and crossed to the old property map on the wall. He pointed to a spot. The graveyard. "This is all of the camp's area."

"White Bear bought the graveyard?" Nick asked. "Why?"

Patrick shook his head. "This is a really old map."

"What are you saying? That camp always owned the graveyard?"

Patrick shrugged. "I guess. I mean, this is an actual surveyor's map."

"It *is* part of this property," Bartholomew confirmed.

"Did Gillian know that?" Abby asked.

"She must have," Patrick shrugged. "It's on her wall."

"We're getting off topic," Erik said, annoyed. "How do we disrupt the ritual and get out of here? Do we just stay away from the graveyard?"

"That would disrupt the ritual. Yes," Bartholomew said. "The last two avoid being killed."

Erik gestured at the small creature in a *see* gesture.

"How long do we need to avoid the monsters," Abby asked.

"Twenty-four hours after the first of you arrived. The camp will return to your real world."

A glance at their watches.

"I assume Gillian doesn't count since she is always here," Patrick said, pulling his phone out. "Me and Nick got here a bit before noon. Maybe eleven-thirty, that gives us another hour and a half."

"No," Abby said.

"No?"

"Ben was here before you."

"Oh, shit. You're right. Anyone know when he arrived?"

"Just Ben himself," Nick said, "and maybe Gillian. Unless his arrival doesn't count because he left camp property."

They looked to Bartholomew who shrugged.

"So worst case we need to avoid them an hour and a half," Patrick said. "Good."

"We barricade ourselves somewhere safe then," Erik added

"Safe?" Abby said. "Where's that?"

No answer.

"Hold on." Nick raised one hand, getting a feeling like they were missing an important point. "Bartholomew, what happens to us when camp returns to the real world?"

The little gnomish creature nodded. "You all stay here. Forever. In a nightmare version of your camp."

"Well, that's just fucking great," Erik said. "Were you gonna tell us about that?"

Bartholomew shrugged again.

"What other options are there?" Nick asked. "How else do we disrupt this ritual?"

"Yeah," Erik said. "Spit it out shorty."

Bartholomew's teeth bared briefly at the insult. "The only other way is you kill Lord Nightmare before he kills the last of you."

"Great," Nick said.

Patrick ran one hand down his face. "Anything else we need to know?"

"I got one," Nick said. "How do we kill Lord Nightmare?"

The four turned toward Bartholomew who was nodding as if expecting the question. "I don't know."

THIRTY-SIX

"For fuck's sake," Erik exploded.

He looked ready to bring the hammer down on Bartholomew.

"Hold on," Patrick said. "How did Lord Nightmare kill your friends."

"With iron."

"Iron?" Abby said. "Like the way fairy-folk are killed?"

The others looked at her and she shrugged. "I have four kids, with a wide variety of interests."

"Iron," Erik said, hefting the hammer. "Got that!"

"We have the weapon," Nick said looking out the door at the shadows moving about. "How the hell do we get to the graveyard?"

"The shadows will harass you," Bartholomew told them, "but they should leave you be as long as you continue toward the graveyard."

"Should?" Patrick asked.

"What do I know, really? If you are in line with fulfilling the prophecy you should be allowed passage."

Should, again.

"Let's find out," Erik said. "Just go out swinging?"

"That won't work," Patrick said. "You can't get all the shadows at once."

"No? Let's see."

Erik rushed to the door and out, down the steps to stand on the edge of the upper compound. The hammer was held in one fist, the head of it resting in his opposite palm.

"Come on then!"

Come closer.

Come with us.

Join us.

"Fuck yourselves."

A hiss of annoyance but the shadows kept their distance, collecting at the side heading toward the dining hall but leaving the opposite direction clear. A message on which way they were permitted to go. Erik glanced left and right, at the ready.

When nothing happened Nick and Patrick followed, Bartholomew on their heels, wringing his hands and glancing at the gathered shadows. Abby came up last, then rushed past Bartholomew to stand with Nick.

Come nearer.

Come to us.

The shadows continued their whispers but didn't approach.

Nick's gaze showed resignation. Abby just looked terrified, but she shrugged.

"I couldn't do this alone," she said, "but with all of you…"

"You are running out of time," Bartholomew warned.

"Shorty is right. Come on," Erik said, taking the lead, hammer balanced against his right shoulder, held by one hand. "Let's do it."

Erik seemed much more animated, more resolved.

"Bet Theo would have made a story about you," Patrick said.

"You think so?"

The path chosen, their task clear, the five turned toward the route which would lead to the graveyard. It was a simple one. Out one side of the camp and follow an increasingly narrow path until it was barely two people wide.

Erik turned his back to the group and continued on with a swagger, the others following.

It felt rushed. Ill-advised. Hasty.

What other option did they have?

Ten minutes passed, each one feeling like it could be their last.

"Hey, shorty," Erik called. "Why don't you come up here and direct me."

Bartholomew passed Patrick and headed to the front, grumbling as he went. The narrowing path brought the shadows in closer. Closer. Closer. Until it felt like they whispered directly into each of their ears.

Come closer.

Step from the path.

Erik jerked the hammer from his shoulder and swung at one shadow to his left. It connected with a shower of sparks and a hiss.

All the shadows screamed.

"No!" Abby said, backing away. "No, no, no!"

She turned, retreating the way they'd come.

"Abby," Nick warned. "Stop!"

"I can't do this…I'm sorry."

She passed Nick and he grabbed her by one arm, gentle but firm.

"Please, Nick. Let me go."

"I can't."

Abby let out a scream. One shadowy hand had latched onto her shoulder. Another reached for her side. Another scream. More shadowed movements.

"Please," she begged.

Nick jerked her by the arm he held, spinning Abby in a half circle so that their positions were reversed. She stumbled back toward Patrick while the shadows fell on Nick.

He screamed.

"Nick!" Abby screamed. She raised her flashlight and pointed it into the shadows, forcing them back.

They seemed to resist more than before but finally they retreated.

The path was empty.

The shadows were gone, and so was Nick.

"No!" she said. "No!"

The others stopped, staring where their friend had been a moment ago.

"Nick!" Patrick yelled. "Nick!"

"He is gone," Bartholomew explained.

"No," Patrick shook his head, refusing to accept it.

"I am afraid so." The little gnomish creature turned back toward the trail. "That is eleven. One left."

They continued on. Patrick leaned close to Abby, whispering comforting words to her as they walked. Ahead Erik leaned toward Bartholomew.

"Hey, shorty," he said in a low voice. "What happens if Lord Nightmare doesn't kill the last sacrifice?"

"As I explained, the ritual fails. The camp returns and you are all trapped here."

"Not what I mean," Erik looked behind at Patrick and Abby in their own conversation. "What if someone *else* kills the last sacrifice?"

Bartholomew glanced at Erik, then considered it a moment. "That person would fulfil the prophecy."

"And?"

"And they would get the prophecy's reward."

"Infinite power."

"For a finite period."

"Good to know," Erik said. "Good to know."

The graveyard appeared all of a sudden and the four stumbled into a clearing. Ancient, weather-worn stones that had long ago lost their names and dates dotted the clearing.

"God!" Abby cried.

Patrick nodded in agreement, unable to find his voice.

Arranged around the graveyard, floating above individual gravestones were the characters they'd all known. King Raccoon. Lady Tadpole. Fancy Nancy. The Woodsman. The Crying Boy. Four of the Fluffies. Ike and Spike. And arranged around the outside of the graveyard, ringing its far end was the huge aquatic monster, Leviticus.

At the center of the graveyard was the same table from the dining hall with all of their friends assembled around it. One seat remained empty. Lisa had now joined them, hacked apart. Nick was more shadow than human, skin turned black with their touch. The rest sat in the same arrangement. Theo with his severed arm. Gillian face down. Miles and Rob leaning against each other.

"No," Abby whispered.

The useless gun was in her hand, like a placebo.

Erik recovered first, turning back toward Abby and Patrick, a strange gleam in his eye.

"Eleven down." He raised his hammer. "One to go."

"No!" Patrick said, one hand raised. He took a step forward.

Abby brought the gun up.

Erik laughed at the futile attempt. He'd decided to take out Patrick. Abby would be easier to control afterwards.

The gun pointed at his face as the hammer started its arc.

BLAM!

A bloody hole appeared in the center of Erik's forehead. A look of surprise as the light in his eyes went out. He toppled backward into the dirt and dandelions of the graveyard.

Patrick turned in shock to Abby.

"I told them they didn't know anything about guns."

"Abby... How...?"

"I found one bullet on Gillian's desk and picked it up."

"You were lucky it was for the right gun."

"What other one could it be?"

Patrick shook his head.

"No one even saw me load it."

She threw the now for sure empty weapon down on Erik. The two looked around.

"Are we back in the real world?" Patrick asked.

"We're not," Bartholomew answered.

They turned to the little man who glanced around him, confused.

"You should have the power now," he said to Abby. "You fulfilled the prophecy."

"What is going on Bartholomew?" Patrick demanded.

"I don't know. The twelfth sacrifice should have ended it all."

"Unless you're working for Lord Nightmare?" Patrick demanded.

Abby gasped. "Was this all a ruse to get us here?"

"No!" Bartholomew spat. "Why would I work with him? He killed my brothers. He killed my friends."

"Ahem," a voice said from behind.

The three spun to see Gillian standing at the table, hunting rifle pointed at them. The missing one from Claude's wall.

"He isn't working with Lord Nightmare," she said. "I am."

Then she shot Bartholomew.

THIRTY-SEVEN

"No!" Patrick yelled, catching the little creature's falling body.

He was already gone.

Abby looked from Gillian to the handgun resting on Erik's dead body.

"Go ahead," Gillian said. "We both know its empty."

"Gillian?" Patrick said, clearly still not believing his eyes. His mind whirled. When they'd seen her body at the table, in the dining hall, she'd been alive? Lying there, faking? "You're behind this? Why?"

"To fulfil the prophecy."

"But why?"

The rifle lowered slightly, not so much that it couldn't be pointed directly at either one in a blink.

"For camp."

"I don't—"

"We're bankrupt, Patrick. One more season and we'll be selling camp off to property developers. I'm desperate."

"Broke? But the donations."

"Even with donations and government grants we fall short every year. The debts continue to grow. These kids and their families are low-income, at-risk people who can't afford the difference. We do good work here!"

"Yes, but—"

"Seven hundred kids every summer. More than fourteen thousand since we all started working here. Camp White Bear is so necessary."

"I don't deny kids need this camp."

"And I... need Lord Nightmare to save it."

"Why?"

"The final sacrifice will give us the power to save camp."

"How?"

Gillian looked confused, glanced aside, shook her head. "With that power Lord Nightmare will save the camp. We'll have the money we need."

"Why sacrifice us?" Abby jumped in. "We were friends!"

Gillian looked embarrassed, ashamed. "I'm sorry. It needed to be personal, a true sacrifice. It wouldn't have been the same with twelve random townies from Millersville."

"Is that what Lord Nightmare told you?"

More confusion. "He... Yes, he did. He came to me in my dreams. He told me about the prophecy. I resisted at first but—"

"But you needed to save the camp."

"Yes! You get it Pat."

"I get it."

"You get it?!" Abby looked at him with a stunned expression before rounding on Gillian. "From my count eleven of us are gone, with your cook and handyman. So which one of us gets shot here?"

"I get it, Gillian," Patrick repeated, drawing her attention back to him. "But I ask you again: You trust him?"

"I... have to."

"Do you? Theo's stories didn't have Lord Nightmare as the most trustworthy character."

"Theo! They weren't even his stories. They came from the magic of this mountain. Theo was just a conduit."

"Then the stories were true."

"They... Yes, they would have to be."

"Do you not remember the story about Lord Nightmare that he told us? The story he only told once."

Gillian thought back, nodded.

"A trickster. A liar. Is that the kind of creature you can trust?"

Gillian's voice was low, quavering. "I have to, Pat. The camp..."

"Why would he save White Bear once he has the power?"

"I—"

"Lord Nightmare will be free in the real world."

"No. That isn't the deal."

"What is the deal?"

"I bring him twelve sacrifices. He fulfills the prophecy, and uses his power to save the camp. He needs the camp too. Lord Nightmare feeds on the children's dreams."

"Why would he need it with a world full of children?"

"I... I..."

A roiling blackness entered the graveyard, black as soot, thick and noxious. The black folded inward, drawing the shadows to it until a form could be realized. When it was done the hulking image of Lord Nightmare stood to one side of the table. It was living blackness up to the face which hid inside an ancient warrior's helmet. All that could be discerned there were two yellowish eyes and a fanged mouth.

"Why do you hesitate, Gillian?" it rumbled.

"I have questions, Lord Nightmare," she spat out. It was an obvious effort to get the words free. Like she was fighting an outside influence.

The voice chuckled. "A little late, don't you think?"

"I should have questioned long ago. Will you save the camp?"

"I have every intention of passing beyond this mountain and feeding on the nightmares of the world."

"You said—"

"I lied."

"But—"

"Don't worry, your precious camp will be saved."

"No. I—"

"Let this be ended," Lord Nightmare commanded. "Choose one, and I will destroy them."

Gillian looked to Patrick and Abby, as if telling them to run. From the shadows behind them stepped other shapes, cutting off all escape. The axe-man. Doris, the crazy cook. The Wendigo. Several doppelgangers, constantly shifting appearance. Many shadows, filling the gaps in between them all.

"There is no escape for them. Choose Gillian."

"Why does she have to choose?" Patrick asked. "Why don't you do it?"

"This is the cost, to save her precious camp."

"Save it?" Gillian demanded. "Save it for what? If the rest of the world is destroyed."

Another chuckle.

"Patrick, I'm sor—"

"Patrick?" Lord Nightmare rumbled the name, like a thunderclap. "Very well."

"No!" Gillian screamed. "I didn't mean that."

Lord Nightmare surged forward and Patrick scrambled toward Erik's body. He grabbed the sledge hammer and brought it up as Lord Nightmare descended on him. The iron connected with the deep blackness of the monster, sparks flying. The hammer's head melted away.

"Arghhh!!!!!" Lord Nightmare yelled.

A moment of complete silence.

Then the monster chuckled.

"You hurt me, I will admit that."

"No." Patrick tried to back-pedal away. "No."

"For that indignity I will kill you both."

The other creatures closed in on Patrick and Abby.

"No!" Gillian repeated, more strength in her voice. "Wait."

The circle continued to close around the two as they stood back-to-back, waiting for the end.

Then... the sound of a rifle cocking.

Lord Nightmare laughed again. "That will do no harm to

me, Gillian. Even if the bullets were iron. The best you could do is kill one of them before I do."

"Which would give me the power."

"That will not happen, Gillian," Lord Nightmare said. With a gesture the hulking form of the axe-man was positioned between Gillian and the remaining two friends. "And for defying me I think I will destroy your precious camp too."

His continued toward Patrick and Abby.

BLAM!

A deep thunderous chuckle

Lord Nightmare turned toward Gillian, a caustic comment on his lips.

It died stillborn.

Gillian remained at the table. The rifle barrel was placed under her chin, smoke billowing from between her skin and the metal. The top of her head had been removed by the rifle's bullet passage.

"No." This time the voice of Lord Nightmare was a whisper.

Gillian collapsed back into her chair.

Abby stared at the spectacle with a sort of grim satisfaction before turning to Patrick. "What's that supposed to do?"

The monsters remained.

Lord Nightmare remained.

Patrick stared past her.

A glow, like sunrise on the horizon seeped from Gillian. Her body was drawn upward, past where she could have stood, hovering above the chair where she'd died. Her face and head were a mask of bloody gore.

"Gillian?" Patrick said.

"Yes."

"The prophecy," Lord Nightmare hissed.

"Oh yes," Gillian confirmed.

The light raced through the graveyard, banishing the monsters, the shadows, back into the darkness.

"You lied to me," Gillian said to Lord Nightmare.

"And you tricked me," he replied.

She didn't answer.

"Ah well," he said. "Back to the dreamlands."

"Not for you." Gillian waved a hand and Lord Nightmare's form disintegrated, starting at his feet.

Lord Nightmare looked down. "No! Don't!"

Gillian glowed with the power of the final sacrifice, of the prophecy fulfilled. "You are far too powerful continue on."

In a rush the darkness of Lord Nightmare's form was replaced with light, destroying the evil creature.

Gillian turned to Patrick and Abby.

"You're some sort of god now?" Abby asked, the contempt in her voice clear.

"For a very limited time," Gillian confirmed. "Already I am fading away."

"Gillian—"

"No time Patrick, let me speak. I only have a minute," she rushed on, speaking quick as the light inside her expanded. It was as if she were building to some critical mass. "I've saved the camp. It's all I ever wanted. There is money for everything in the office."

"Why not bring back our dead friends?" Abby asked.

"I can't. The sacrifice is necessary. To reverse it would

just start the whole thing again." She turned to Patrick. "Look after camp. The deed is in your name now."

"I think she's talking to you," Abby said.

"Yeah, I got that," Patrick shrugged. "Of course. But who will send their kids to a camp where twelve people got murdered?"

Gillian had become blinding to look on. Both Patrick and Abby averted their gaze. Gillian's voice became thin, as if shouting from the other end of a long tunnel.

"I took care of that too."

EPILOGUE

"Now, each summer the brass bell is rung twelve times," Miguel said.

He'd been a counsellor for three years now, ever since Patrick took it over.

The kids around the campfire listened, hanging on his words.

"Twelve times at the start of summer. One for each of the beloved characters. King Raccoon. Lady Tadpole. Ike. Spike. Bartholomew, and all of the others."

Patrick listened from one side. He loved this story, had actually been the one to tell Miguel about it. The characters would live on in the stories they told.

"And twelve times at the end, for past staff no longer with us."

This was his acknowledgement to the sacrifice of his friends. They had no choice in it but he could honor them at the least.

As Gillian had returned them and camp to the real world, in her final desperate moments, she had whipped up a freak storm. It ripped through the area, doing little damage to the property, but taking with it twelve people from a reunion. No bodies were ever found.

"And the bright lady continues to watch over camp, to protect us all against the likes of those dark creatures out there... but theirs is a tale for the nighttime."

ABOUT THE AUTHOR

John T. Haas, a Canadian author from Montreal, spent twelve great years in Calgary before settling in Ottawa, though he still longs for those Rocky Mountains. Writing is his lifelong passion, but he started pursuing publishing seriously after his sons were born. Since then, he's had over thirty short stories published and authored seven novels and three anthologies. His humorous fantasy trilogy starts with "The Reluctant Barbarian." After winning the Writer's of the Future contest in 2019 with his novella "The Damned Voyage," he launched a prequel Lovecraftian trilogy with "Cults of Death and Madness," published by Wordfire Press. He also has a standalone horror novel, "Stay Out." John aims to be a full-time writer, dreaming of fame and fortune, but taking it step by step. He lives with his supportive family, who inspire and motivate him to keep writing.

Also by John T. Haas

<u>The Midnight Library Collection</u>

Stay Out!

Camp Nightmare

~

<u>Book of Ancient Evil Series</u>

Cults of Death and Madness

Book Of Death and Madness

Prophet of Death and Madness

~

<u>Impossible Quests</u>

The Reluctant Barbarian

The Wayward Spider

Unavoidable Quests

~

<u>Anthologies</u>

Whispers- Collected Tales of Horror

Echoes - Collected Tales of Fantasy and Mystery

Enigmas - Collected Tales of Science-Fiction

www.ingramcontent.com/pod-product-compliance
Lightning Source LLC
Chambersburg PA
CBHW032002050726
47590CB00006B/2018